Chinese-English Version

Lush Mountains as Witnesses

Written by Xu Qiren

Translated by Hao Tugen, Wang Qiaoying & Huang Quancan

（英汉对照本）

青山鉴

徐启仁　著

郝涂根　王巧英　黄全灿　译

全国百佳图书出版单位

APCTIME 时代出版

时代出版传媒股份有限公司

黄山书社

图书在版编目(CIP)数据

青山鉴:英汉对照本/徐启仁著;郝涂根,王巧英,黄全灿译.—合肥:黄山书社,2021.4
ISBN 978-7-5461-7358-0

Ⅰ.①青… Ⅱ.①徐… ②郝… ③王… ④黄… Ⅲ.①黄梅戏-剧本-中国-当代-汉、英 Ⅳ.①I236.54

中国版本图书馆 CIP 数据核字(2021)第 084289 号

青 山 鉴
QING SHAN JIAN

徐启仁 著
郝涂根 王巧英 黄全灿 译

出 品 人 贾兴权
责任编辑 徐娟娟 熊裕娟
装帧设计 李 昕
责任印制 李 磊
出版发行 黄山书社(http://www.hspress.cn)
地址邮编 安徽省合肥市蜀山区翡翠路 1118 号出版传媒广场 7 层 230071
印 刷 安徽联众印刷有限公司
版 次 2022 年 4 月第 1 版
印 次 2022 年 4 月第 1 次印刷
开 本 880 mm × 1230 mm 1/32
字 数 150 千字
印 张 5.5
书 号 ISBN 978-7-5461-7358-0
定 价 39.00 元

服务热线 0551-63533706
销售热线 0551-63533761
官方直营书店(https://hsss.tmall.com)

谨以此书纪念已故著名黄梅戏国家二级编剧徐启仁先生

In commemoration of Mr. Xu Qiren,
the late famous national second-grade scenarist of Huangmei Opera

徐启仁简介

徐启仁（1946.8—2018.4），安徽桐城人，国家二级编剧。1960年高小毕业后进剧团学艺，先后在近百部大小剧目中担任主要角色。

20世纪80年代中期开始剧本创作，主要作品有大戏《左光斗》《遗祸》《胭脂湖》《傲骨寒梅》《绿鹦哥》《青山鉴》等六部，小戏《村姑与乾隆》《醉酒》《尚板眼与麻二姑》《锦儿》四出，其中四出小戏在《剧本》月刊上刊出。其作品曾获省戏剧节展览演出奖、“田汉戏剧奖”剧本二等奖、省规划题材创作二等奖、中国戏剧文学奖剧本奖、第四届黄梅戏艺术节金黄梅奖、省黄梅戏基金会剧本奖等奖项。小戏《村姑与乾隆》在中国剧协主办的2004年“中国曹禺戏剧奖”小品、小戏评选中，获优秀编剧奖，同时获得专业组剧目一等奖、中央电视台优秀剧目奖。

徐启仁先生担任过剧团艺委会负责人、演出队长、剧团团长等职，当选过桐城市政协委员。曾是中国戏剧文学学会会员、安徽剧协会员、安庆剧协理事、桐城市戏剧家协会主席。

（以上剧照均由应尼摄影提供）

目 录

前 言 …… 1
剧情简介 …… 2
剧中人物表 …… 6
序幕 …… 8
第一场 …… 14
第二场 …… 46
第三场 …… 70
第四场 …… 88
第五场 …… 122
第六场 …… 136
第七场 …… 148
注 释 …… 162

Contens

Preface ········· 3
Synopsis ········· 3
Characters ········· 7
Prelude ········· 9
Act Ⅰ ········· 15
Act Ⅱ ········· 47
Act Ⅲ ········· 71
Act Ⅳ ········· 89
Act Ⅴ ········· 123
Act Ⅵ ········· 137
Act Ⅶ ········· 149
Notes ········· 162

前　言

《青山鉴》是由已故著名剧作家徐启仁先生创作、安徽省桐城市黄梅戏剧团于2015年创作演出的新编现代大型黄梅戏，为第七届中国（安庆）黄梅戏艺术节参演剧目。曾荣获第二十八届“田汉戏剧奖”剧本类二等奖和2015年安徽省黄梅戏新剧目展演“优秀剧目奖”。2017年，《青山鉴》作为安徽省和黄梅戏剧种的唯一入选剧目，登上北京长安大戏院舞台，参加由中宣部、文化部主办的全国基层院团戏曲会演。

该剧讲述了两个林业专业的大学毕业生——章兰兰和周立凡为建设美好乡村，返乡创业办林场，携手奉献青春和汗水的故事，颂扬了当代青年有理想、有抱负、有担当的精神，表达了绿水青山就是金山银山的主题。

为了更好地“讲述中国故事”，坚定文化自信，向海外展现习近平“两山”理论对中国当代青年积极投身美好乡村建设的影响，因此，对新编现代黄梅戏剧目《青山鉴》进行中英对照翻译，既能消除语言障碍，加深中国和“一带一路”沿线国家的文化交流与合作，又能帮助他们了解中国当代青年的精神风貌和中国美好乡村建设的近况。

作为安徽省教育厅人文社科研究重点项目“黄梅戏经典剧目英语译介研究”，以及安庆师范大学外国语学院“关联理论指导下的大学英语翻译教学研究”和“临床实践型英语教师培养的路径与机制研究”等项目的阶段性成果，新编现代黄梅戏剧目《青山鉴》的翻译力求“达意”“传神”，同时注重剧本中唱词念白的可阅读性和可演唱性。为方便中外读者阅读及理解，译者对剧本中有中国文化特色的名称、典故、习语、俗语、歇后语、诗词等作了英文注释；同时严格按照中文字数确定英文的音节数，确保英语译文可以根据曲调演唱。全书采用中英对照的形式排版，并附部分剧照，以供读者欣赏。

参与本书翻译的有郝涂根、王巧英、黄全灿和安庆师范大学外国语学院2019级翻译硕士。郝涂根对该剧本的英译给予了指导，并带队访问桐城市黄梅戏剧团，与该剧编剧、已故著名黄梅戏编剧徐启仁先生之子徐雷先生，就《青山鉴》的创作初衷和立意进行了探讨，为该译著的翻译和出版提供了巨大的帮助；王巧英对译稿进行了反复修改与润色，翻译注释、撰写前言并对全文进行排版；黄全灿全面组织、协调翻译工作，审核全文并翻译前言；2019级翻译硕士参与本译著前期翻译，其中罗天星同学表现较为突出。

本译著得到了安徽省桐城市黄梅戏剧团的大力支持，他们无偿提供了《青山鉴》进京汇报演出的剧本及剧照；徐启仁先生之子徐雷先生无偿提供了《青山鉴》剧本并授权同意翻译；黄山书社有关同志对本译著的编辑与出版付出了辛勤的劳动。借此机会对他们一并表示诚挚的感谢。

鉴于译者的知识水平和所掌握的黄梅戏翻译资料有限，书中难免存在错误和不妥之处，恳请专家和读者批评指正。

译　者

2021年1月27日

Preface

Lush Mountains as Witnesses, a modern Huangmei Opera drama written by the late Mr. Xu Qiren, was firstly presented by Tongcheng Municipal Huangmei Opera Troupe in 2015. It was one of the key operas of the 7th China Anqing Huangmei Opera Art Festival in 2015 and was awarded the second prize for script at the 28th Tian Han Drama Award and an Excellent Drama Award at the 2015 New Huangmei Opera Exhibition of Anhui Province. *Lush Mountains as Witnesses* was even presented as the only program from Anhui Province and the only huangmei opera drama at the national drama exhibition jointly held by the Publicity Department of the Communist Party of China and the Ministry of Culture at Beijing Chang'an Grand Theatre in 2017.

Lush Mountains as Witnesses tells a moving and inspiring story of Zhang Lanlan and Zhou Lifan, two forestry graduates starting their business in building a tree farm in their hometown. The love and striving of the two young entrepreneurs display the aspiration, ambition and commitment of modern young Chinese as well as President Xi Jinping's idea that "lucid waters and lush mountains are invaluable assets".

Lush Mountains as Witnesses is chosen by our translation team to better communicate the impact on modern China of President Xi Jinping's idea that "lucid waters and lush mountains are invaluable assets" and to tell China stories better and make Chinese values better understood overseas. We are firmly confident that the publication of the bilingual version of this modern Huangmei drama will help foster cultural communication and cooperation between China and countries along the Belt and Road and better communicate the aspiration of modern Chinese youths in building beautiful countryside in the new era.

The English version of *Lush Mountains as Witnesses* is also a phased result of "A study on the English Translation and Introduction of Classical Repertoire of Huangmei Opera", a key project of the Humanities and Social Sciences Research of the Education Bureau of Anhui Province, and of two research projects implemented at the School of Foreign Languages of Anqing Normal University, namely "College English Translation Teaching Research under the Guidance of Relevance Theory" and "Research on the Route and Mechanism of the Training of Practice-oriented English Teachers". With expressiveness as the general strategy, the translation of *Lush Mountains as Witnesses* focuses on the readability of the spoken parts and singability of the lyrics. For easier and better understanding of the drama, we also offer adequate additional contents such as illustrations, stage photos and detailed notes of typical Chinese proper names, allusions, idioms, proverbs, poems and Chinese two-part allegorical sayings. For quicker imitating and spreading of Huangmei Opera among foreign audience, we translate each line of the lyrics considering the corresponding of syllables in the Chinese and the English language.

The translation of *Lush Mountains as Witnesses* is conducted by the translation team from the School of Foreign Languages of Anqing Normal University, including Professor Hao Tugen, the leader and the chief translator, associate professor Wang Qiaoying, associate professor Huang Quancan and the Grade 2019 master' s candidates of translation and interpreting of the School. Professor Hao, who oversees the whole project, provides all-round guidance to the translation of the drama with his expertise in literature translation. associate professor Wang Qiaoying does most of manuscript translation, working diligently on each step of the whole translation from source text proofreading to translating, revising, polishing, annotating and DTP. Associate Professor Huang Quancan manages the translation project. He also conducts the final revision, polishes the translation, and translates the preface. The Grade 2019 master' s candidates of translation and interpreting take part in the editing, DTP and translating of the drafting version, and Luo Tianxing, one of the MTI students, contributes a lot in the translation of the first three episodes.

Upon the publication of *Lush Mountains as Witnesses*, we would like to express our thanks for the great support from Tongcheng Municipal Huangmei Opera Troupe in offering the Beijing exhibition performance version of the drama as well as the precious stage photos at the Beijing Chang'an Grand Theatre. Additionally, we should say thank-you to Mr. Xu Lei, who kindly grants the permit of the translation of *Lush Mountains as Witnesses* to us and generously offers instant guidance to us in the translation. Furthermore, we should express our sincerest respect and gratitude to Mr. Xu Qiren, whose great works encourage so many of us for so many years and even in the future. Finally, we should express our deepest gratitude and admiration for expertise, keen insight and arduous work of the editing and revising team of the Huangshan Publishing House.

Nonetheless, we still feel there might be a huge space for the improvement of the translation of the drama. We sincerely welcome valuable advice and suggestions to us from experts and readers.

The Translators

January 27, 2021

青山鉴

Lush Mountains as Witnesses

剧情简介

两个学林业的大学毕业生,章兰兰和周立凡,因共同的志向走到了一起。

章兰兰放弃家中优越的生活条件,回乡创业,担任金凤林场场长;周立凡不顾家人反对离家出走,来到章兰兰身边携手创业。他们在艰苦的条件下努力工作,共同的理想和追求使这对年轻人相爱了。

一直寻找儿子的周立凡父母想方设法终于找到了儿子。母亲放言:若儿子不回家,她宁愿一死。在章兰兰的劝说下,周立凡又回到了父母身边。但是这对情人已是难舍难分……

章兰兰的为人给周立凡的妹妹周立娜留下了好感,在她的劝说下父母转变了看法。

Synopsis

This is a story of Zhang Lanlan and Zhou Lifan, two university graduates majoring in forestry, falling in love thanks to their common aspiration.

Instead of enjoying comfortable life at home, Zhang Lanlan returned to her hometown to start a business as the director of Jinfeng Tree Farm. Zhou Lifan ran away from home regardless of the opposition of his family and came to join Zhang's business. Despite all hardships and obstacles, they realized their aspiration of building a greener village and fell love in the lush mountains.

Zhou Lifan's parents tried all means to find their son who ran away from home to pursue his dream. The mother warned that she would commit suicide if her son did not return home. Zhou Lifan returned to his parents but the couple found it difficult for them to tear apart...

However, Zhang Lanlan's personality left a good impression on Zhou Lifan's younger sister, Zhou Lina, whose persuasion changed her parents' views.

在一个风雨交加的日子，二人为救护红豆杉幼苗，在山上相遇。雨过天晴，章兰兰向周立凡道出了作为一个女孩子，她为什么要学林业的秘密。

在当地党委、政府的关怀下，金凤林场越办越好；周立凡的父母也主动出资支持林场建设，更加喜欢这位善良能干、漂亮的准儿媳妇。

以章兰兰、周立凡为代表的年轻人，有理想、有抱负、有担当。他们自主创业，为了祖国的绿化事业，挥洒着青春的汗水，他们用实际行动，诠释了习近平总书记的话：绿水青山就是金山银山。

On a stormy day, the two met on the mountain when trying to rescue the yew seedlings. After the storm calmed down, Zhang Lanlan told Zhou Lifan why she as a woman had forestry as her job.

Under the guidance and support from the local government and CPC committee as well as the funding from Zhou Lifan's parents, Jinfeng Tree Farm boomed.

Zhang Lanlan and Zhou Lifan, representatives of modern Chinese youths with ideals, ambitions, and responsibilities, started their own businesses and worked diligently for the greening of the motherland. Their striving best interprets the famous remark by General Secretary Xi Jinping that "lucid waters and lush mountains are invaluable assets."

剧中人物表

章兰兰:女,二十二岁,网名“芳草”。林学院毕业,回乡创办金凤林场。

周立凡:男,二十三岁,网名“天马”。林业大学毕业生。

周立娜:周立凡之妹,大专生,二十岁。

刘惠芹:周立凡之母,四十多岁。

周志豪:周立凡之父,近五十岁,民营水产公司老板。

谢主任:男,近四十岁,青山村村主任。

章五姑:近四十岁,凭“智力”挣钱的女人。

彩　霞:女,二十岁,林场员工,章兰兰好友。

章七爷:男,七十多岁,章兰兰祖父。

哑　婶:女,五十多岁,哑巴,林场炊事员。

巧　珍:女,二十多岁。

二顺子:男,二十多岁。

三春、梅花、秀姑、爱莲:林场青年女员工。

Characters

Zhang Lanlan, female, 22 years old, with a screen name "Fangcao", a graduate who returned home to establish Jinfeng Tree Farm.

Zhou Lifan, male, 23 years old, with a screen name "Tianma", a forestry graduate.

Zhou Lina, Zhou Lifan's younger sister, a 20-year-old junior college student.

Liu Huiqin, Zhou Lifan's mother, in her 40s.

Zhou Zhihao, Zhou Lifan's father, in his late 40s, the owner of a private fishery company.

Director Xie, male, in his late 30s, the village committee director of Qingshan Village.

Zhang Wugu, female, in her late 30s, who earns money by "intelligence".

Caixia, female, 20 years old, an employee of the tree farm and a good friend of Zhang Lanlan.

Zhang Qiye, male, in his 70s, grandfather of Zhang Lanlan.

Yashen, female, in her 50s, a cook of the tree farm who cannot speak because of a disability.

Qiaozhen, female, in her 20s.

Ershunzi, male, in his 20s.

Sanchun, Meihua, Xiugu, Ailian, young female staff of the tree farm.

序　幕

时间　现代。

地点　安徽江北某市。

（合唱）山青青，水盈盈，
大地劲吹世纪风。
男儿的追寻，
女儿的憧憬，
为圆那绿色的梦，
定格那满眼的春。

［幕启　舞台后光区左右周立凡章兰兰各手执一台平板电脑。

章兰兰　天马，谢谢你。你做的林场规划设计图太棒了！林业局工程师说这是专家水平。

周立凡　芳草，过奖了！是你提供的图片和资料扎实、详尽，我才能完成设计。你满意吗？说真话！

Prelude

Time　　Modern

Place　　A city in the north of the Yangtze River of Anhui Province

(chorus) Lush mountains, shiny waters, and
The wind from the new century.
A man's pursuit and
A woman's vision
Are to fulfill the green dream
Of a world with eyeful spring.

[The curtain rises. Zhou Lifan and Zhang Lanlan each hold a tablet computer standing on the left and right side of the lighted area in the rear of the stage.

Zhang Lanlan　Tianma, what a great plan blueprint of the tree farm you've made! The engineer of the Forestry Bureau said it must be made by an expert.

Zhou Lifan　Fangcao, you're flattering me! It's the detailed information and vivid pictures you've provided that help me complete the plan. Do you like it? Tell me the truth!

章兰兰　满意！和我设想的不谋而合，太不可思议了！

周立凡　心有灵犀一点通嘛！

章兰兰　天马，设计费是多少？照直说。

周立凡　你刚刚创业，处处都要钱，算我为你尽义务！设计费免了！

章兰兰　天马，应该尊重你的劳动，你付出了心血呀！

周立凡　芳草，我有一个要求和疑问！

章兰兰　一个要求？一个疑问？请说吧！

周立凡　你是一个女孩子，怎么会爱上林业？那可是个受苦受累、难见成效的事业啊！

章兰兰　我呀，暂时不告诉你，看以后有没有机会！

周立凡　这……

章兰兰　提你的要求吧！

周立凡　芳草，能说出你的真实姓名吗？通过视频我们见见面行吗？

章兰兰　天马，我们不是有过约定吗？在虚拟的世界里，保持点神秘，保持点距离，不是更有意思吗？

周立凡　保持点距离？

Zhang Lanlan Yes, I do! It coincides with my idea. How incredible!

Zhou Lifan It's because our minds think alike.

Zhang Lanlan Tianma, how much is the design fee? Just speak frankly.

Zhou Lifan You've just started your business and need money for it. It's free of charge!

Zhang Lanlan Tianma, your work should be rewarded.

Zhou Lifan Fangcao, I have a question and a request.

Zhang Lanlan A question? And a request? Please go ahead.

Zhou Lifan You are a girl, how could you fall in love with forestry? It was a painful and difficult job!

Zhang Lanlan I... won't tell you the reason for the time being. Let me see if I could tell you why in the future!

Zhou Lifan Well...

Zhang Lanlan Now make your request!

Zhou Lifan Fangcao, can you tell me your real name now? Can we see each other through the video?

Zhang Lanlan Tianma, didn't we make a promise? Isn't it more interesting to keep some mystery and a little distance in the virtual world?

Zhou Lifan Keep a little distance?

章兰兰　对,保持点距离!

周立凡　芳草,我们已经是老朋友了,相处这么长时间了!

章兰兰　喂,哪个和你相处啦!

周立凡　在网上不也是相处吗?我真想走进你的生活,和你一起种树搞研究,行吗?

章兰兰　天马,现在还不行。我们这儿很苦,真的很苦,苦得你会整天哭鼻子[1]的。我这个林场场长还要专门派个人来哄你开心呢。

周立凡　我喜欢这一行!我真的不怕吃苦!

章兰兰　天马,等我忙过这阵子再说吧!

周立凡　芳草,我会找到你的!

章兰兰　天马,再见!我关机了!

周立凡　芳草,我会找到你的!

[切光。黑暗中听到周立凡呼喊:“芳草,我会找到你的!”

Zhang Lanlan Yeah, keep a distance!

Zhou Lifan Fangcao, we've been old friends and have got along with each other for such a long time!

Zhang Lanlan Hey, who has got along with you?

Zhou Lifan Haven't we got along with on the internet? Fangcao, I really want to join in your life, plant trees and do research with you. Is it OK?

Zhang Lanlan Tianma, not now. Our life is very tough, truly tough, even tough enough to make you a crybaby[1]. I, the director of the tree farm, may have to send someone to keep you happy.

Zhou Lifan I love this business! I really am not afraid of hardship!

Zhang Lanlan Tianma, wait until I'm not busy.

Zhou Lifan Fangcao, I'll find you!

Zhang Lanlan Tianma, Goodbye. I'll shut down my computer!

Zhou Lifan Fangcao, I'll find you!

[Light switches. Zhou Lifan was heard shouting in the dark: "Fangcao, I'll find you!"

第一场

[初夏。

[连绵起伏的山峦,裸露出大片的山体。星星点点的苍松翠柏,格外葱绿。

[山路旁竖立的大石头上写着“金凤林场”四个大字。此处搭有凉棚,摆着粗糙桌凳。

[谢主任夹只公文包上。

谢主任　去你个绊脚石!

谢主任　(唱)小小村官称九品,
　　　　　　头等大事抓脱贫。
　　　　　　找项目,请能人,
　　　　　　费尽周折都落空。
　　　　　　大片山地难利用,
　　　　　　野兔打洞山鸡鸣。

Act Ⅰ

[Early summer.

[Among the rolling hills, vast areas are bare, sprinkled with green pines and cypresses.

[Four Chinese characters are inscribed on a big roadside stone, Jinfeng Tree Farm. Underneath a shade-shed stands a rough set of table and stools.

[Director Xie enters the stage carrying a briefcase under his arm.

Director Xie　Up yours! A stumbling block!

(sing) I'm a grass-roots official
Busy getting rid of poverty.
New projects and able men
Came to nothing at the end.
Vast mountain areas can't be used,
Hares and pheasants here and there.

村里干部头都痛，

谁料想半路上杀出个穆桂英[2]！

章兰兰回乡创业办林场，

大学生不恋城市恋农村。

她有心想干大事业，

会不会一时冲动太天真？

[章七爷提着竹篮上。

谢主任　七爷,你又上山来啦？放心不下你那宝贝孙女吧？

章七爷　不放心哪！你说一个大学生,么事不好找,偏偏要办林场。她爸她妈反对,我也反对,她根本不听,这丫头犟哪！

谢主任　哎,七爷,现在可不能反对了！“金凤林场”是市里支持和肯定的低碳环保项目,又是大学生创业示范项目。镇长刚才给我打电话说,第一笔政府贴息贷款二十万到账了,通知兰兰去办手续。

章七爷　谢主任哪,这钱不能给她！

谢主任　这是为么事啊？

It's such a headache of cadres

That nobody expects a Mu Guiying[2] to come here!

Zhang Lanlan returned to start a business.

A graduate doesn't loves not the city but the country.

She sets her mind on something big.

Will she be too naive to be impulsive?

[Zhang Qiye enters the stage carrying a bamboo basket.

Director Xie Qiye, you're coming up the mountain again. Worry about your baby granddaughter?

Zhang Qiye Yes! Don't you think as a graduate, she can do anything? But she just wants to establish a tree farm! Her parents are against it, and so am I! She didn't listen at all! Alas, what a stubborn girl!

Director Xie Hey, Qiye, now you shouldn't oppose it anymore! Jinfeng Tree Farm is a low-carbon environment-friendly project approved and supported by the municipal government. Moreover, it's a graduate start-up demonstration project. Just now, the town mayor called me to ask Lanlan to handle procedures for the first 200,000-yuan subsidized loan from the government.

Zhang Qiye Director Xie, you can't give her this money by all means!

Director Xie Why not?

章七爷　要是场子办垮了,她拿什么还哪!

谢主任　你孙女心思大呢!她说要把这个林场办成绿色氧吧、花卉基地、乡村公园、休闲度假村。莫说二十万,就是一百万也不够!

章七爷　我种了一辈子林子也没有种出个名堂!当初你们就不应该同意她办林场!

谢主任　兰兰是学林的,这么大一片山地又无人开发,兰兰是替村里做了一件大好事呀!我看兰兰做事还有章有法,说不定能成功!

章七爷　唉,她放着好日子不过,她爸爸在浙江办那么大的厂子,要她去她就是不去,偏要自己创业,这容易吗?看花容易绣花难!

谢主任　青年人创业我能不支持吗?失败了,就算交了学费,你儿子能不管吗?

章七爷　(苦笑)老子挣钱,女儿花钱,也对也对。(对着大山喊)兰兰,爷爷给你煮了茶叶蛋,快来吃呀!

Zhang Qiye If her farm collapses, with what can she pay back?

DirectorXie Your granddaughter is ambitious! She said she wanted to turn this tree farm into a green oxygen bar, a flower base, a countryside park and a leisure resort. Not to mention 200,000 yuan, even a million yuan is not enough for that!

Zhang Qiye I've been planting trees all my life and didn't make it! You guys shouldn't have allowed her to start the tree farm!

DirectorXie Lanlan majored in forestry. Such a vast mountain area remained idle. Lanlan is doing a good deed for the village! In my view, Lanlan is quite methodical in her work. Maybe she could be successful!

Zhang Qiye Alas! She doesn't care for an easy and comfortable life but would rather start an enterprise! Her dad runs such a big factory in Zhejiang and wants her to work there. She refused and went instead to start her own business. Is this easy? Easier said than done!

DirectorXie Can I not support the young to start their businesses? If she fails, just consider a tuition fee. Your son just ignores her?

Zhang Qiye (forced smile) The father makes money for his daughter to spend. Nothing is wrong about that. (yell to the mountain) Lanlan, grandpa has made some tea eggs for you, come and have some!

谢主任　七爷,她听不见。我来。(掏手机拨号码)喂,是兰兰吗?

[章兰兰声音:"谢主任,是我。"

谢主任　兰兰啊!有一个好消息要告诉你

[章兰兰声音:"谢主任,你说。"

谢主任　不急,等你下来再说。哦,你爷爷还有话要对你讲!

章七爷　(接过谢主任的手机)喂,兰兰,你在做么事啊?

[章兰兰声音:"爷爷,我在搞土壤调查!"

章七爷　土壤调查?你找哪个调查呀?爷爷给你煮了茶叶蛋!你快下来吃哦!

[章兰兰声音:"爷爷,你又给我送茶叶蛋啦?就丢在场子门口,你回去吧!"

章七爷　(将手机还给谢主任)土壤还要调查?现在这些年轻人……

(放下篮子往回走)

谢主任　七爷,这叫科学!

章七爷　谢主任,我走了啊!

Director Xie	Qiye, she can't hear you. Let me call her. (take out a phone to dial) Hello, is that Lanlan?

[Zhanglanlan's voice: "Director Xie, it's me."

DirectorXie	Lanlan, I have good news for you!

[Zhang Lanlan's voice: "Director Xie, what is it?"

DirectorXie	Take it easy. I'll wait until you come down. Now, your grandpa has something to tell you. (hand the phone to Zhang Qiye)

Zhang Qiye	(take the phone from Director Xie) Hello, Lanlan, what are you up to now?

[Zhang Lanlan's voice: "Grandpa, I'm working on the soil survey."

Zhang Qiye	Soil survey? Who are you surveying? Grandpa has brought you some tea eggs. Come quickly to have some!

[Zhang Lanlan's voice: "Grandpa, you've come to send tea eggs again? Just leave them at the gate of the farm. You may go back."

Zhang Qiye	(return the phone to Director Xie) Does soil need surveying? These young people ... (put down the basket and go back)

DirectorXie	Qiye, this is called science.

Zhang Qiye	Director Xie, I'm leaving!

谢主任　七爷，下山慢点！

章七爷　谢主任，你真要多费点神哪！

谢主任　七爷，放心，放心啊！

[幕后传来梅花等人的声音："二顺子，站住！""站住！"

[二顺子慌慌张张逃上，与谢主任撞个满怀，二人倒地，梅花等人追上。

谢主任　（火）二顺子，你急着去砍头[3]哇！

二顺子　（忙扶谢主任，赔笑脸）谢主任，后面有老虎追我！

谢主任　老虎，哪有老虎啊？我们村要是有老虎就发着！

众姑娘　二顺子……

谢主任　哎呀！好着，好着！

三　春　谢主任，二顺子尽捣乱！

秀　姑　他老往林场跑，缠着我们胡说八道！

梅　花　他还说要学唐伯虎点秋香[4]。我们上厕所他也跟着！真不要脸！

Director Xie　Qiye, take it easy when going downhill!

Zhang Qiye　Director Xie, would you mind taking care of her?

Director Xie　Qiye, no, I wouldn't. Rest assured!

[Voices of Meihua and others come from behind the curtain: "Ershunzi, stop!" "Stop!"

Ershunzi escapes onto the stage, flustered. He bumps into Director Xie and the two fall on the ground with him. Meihua and others catch up.

Director Xie　(angrily) Ershunzi, are you in a hurry to be beheaded?![3]

Ershunzi　(hurry to help Director Xie up and speak with a flattering smile) Director Xie, there're some tigers chasing after me!

Director Xie　Tigers? Where are the tigers? Our village would get rich if there were any tigers!

Girls　Ershunzi...

Director Xie　Whoops! All right! All right!

Sanchun　Director Xie, Ershunzi is always making trouble!

Xiugu　He's always coming to the tree farm and pestering us with his nonsense!

Meihua　He also said that he would imitate Tang Bohu's way of selecting Qiuxiang[4]. He went so far as to follow us to the toilet! How shameless!

巧　珍　谢主任，你管不管哪？不行我找派出所去！

众姑娘　对，我们找派出所去！

谢主任　哎！二顺子，你这是性骚扰，知道吗？你这是犯法，知道吗？年纪轻轻，游手好闲，还靠娘老子养活，丢不丢人？

二顺子　谢主任，你怎么一点同情心也没有？我，一个大龄光棍，找老婆也犯法啊？

谢主任　有你这样找老婆的吗？死皮赖脸，三牲圆子——硬上[5]！我告诉你，以后没有我的同意，不准随便往林场跑！

众姑娘　对！不准他往林场跑！

二顺子　（不服气）听别人说金凤林场都是美女如云，我看你们是乌龟爬上秤——自称[6]！（指着众姑娘）我能看上你们吗？我看上的是章兰兰，你们场长！等着吃我的喜糖吧！

［姑娘们哈哈大笑。

谢主任　二顺子，你也不屙泡尿照照[7]，章兰兰会看上你吗？她爷爷要是知道了，不把你捶扁才怪呢！

Qiaozhen — Director Xie, will you discipline him or not? If you won't, I'll go to the police station!

Girls — Right. We'll go to the police station!

Director Xie — Hey! Ershunzi, what you did is sexual harassment, you know? This is illegal, you know? Aren't you ashamed of being so young yet idle and sponging off your parents?

Ershunzi — Director Xie, why don't you have any sympathy for me at all? For me, an elder bachelor, is it illegal to look for a wife?

Director Xie — Is this your way of finding a woman for wife? So brazen-faced and tough[5]! Let me tell you — without my words, you are not allowed to go to the tree farm!

Girls — Right! Don't allow him to go to the tree farm!

Ershunzi — (recalcitrant) Hum! I'm told that Jinfeng Tree Farm is crowded with beauties. In my view, you're singing high praises for yourselves[6]! (point at the girls) How can I take a fancy to you? It's Zhang Lanlan, your director of the farm, who I really want to date! Wait for my wedding candies!

[Girls burst into hearty laughter.

Director Xie — Ershunzi, why don't you take a piss to look at yourself[7]? Forget it. Will Zhang Lanlan take a fancy to you? If her grandpa heard what you said, it would be strange if he didn't beat you up!

[众姑娘大喊:“章七爷来啰!”

[二顺子吓得撒腿跑下,姑娘们拍手欢笑。

谢主任　你们这些小丫头啊度量也放大一点,也要理解一点,二顺子人也不坏,想老婆也不是什么大错,人之常情嘛!

[姑娘们又是一阵哄笑。

三　春　二顺子那副馋相,真是可怜又可嫌!

梅　花　男人想女人,谁像他呀,见到小妹[8]眼珠子都快掉下来了!

秀　姑　二顺子说想兰兰是吹牛,其实他相中的不是兰兰。

爱　莲　不是兰兰,那是谁呀?秀姑,你说呀!

秀　姑　这个人远在天边,近在眼前——就是巧珍!

巧　珍　(火)你胡说!我就那么贱了,看我不抽你!(追打秀姑,其他姑娘护着秀姑,姑娘们打成一团)

谢主任　哎呀!好着,好着!

[彩霞上,她带着土壤样本和取土工具。

彩　霞　(阻止,生气)上班时间,打打闹闹像什么样子?兰兰看见了,你们都得挨熊[9]!

[Girls shout: "Here comes Zhang Qiye!"

[Ershunzi runs off the stage in fright. Girls roar with laughter clapping their hands.

Director Xie You little girls, be nice and understanding. Ershunzi is not a bad guy. It's okay for him to want a wife. It's human nature!

[Girls burst into a guffaw again.

Sanchun That shameless look of Ershunzi is truly pitiful and disgusting!

Meihua A man wants a woman. But nobody wants so much like him that his eyeballs are almost falling off at sight of a young woman[8]!

Xiugu Ershunzi was bragging about wanting to date Lanlan. In fact, it's not Lanlan to whom he takes a fancy.

Ailian If it's not Lanlan, who would it be? Xiugu, spit it out!

Xiugu This girl is right here. She is Qiaozhen!

Qiaozhen (annoyed) Nonsense! Am I that cheap?! See if I slap you or not! (chase after Xiugu to beat her while other girls protect her. They are beating in a mess.)

Director Xie Oh dear! All right, all right!

[Caixia enters the stage with a soil sample and collecting tools.

Caixia (stop them in anger) What are you roughhousing during work hours? If Lanlan sees that, she'll jump on you[9]!)

梅　花　彩霞姐，干活的时候，我们都很认真，休息的时候就放松放松嘛！

众　人　这叫有劳有逸！

彩　霞　你们哪！

三　春　还站着干什么？干活！

众　人　是！

（唱）向前进，向前进，战士们责任重，妇女们冤仇深……（笑着一窝蜂似的跑上台阶）

[哑婶背着米，提着一篮子菜上，显然有些累了。

彩　霞　哑婶，我来替你背！（欲取下哑婶背的米）

众姑娘　我来，我来，我来！

哑　婶　啊，啊哦……（比画着哑语，意思自己背得动，又指着篮子里的鲜肉，比画着给大伙儿打牙祭[10]）

彩　霞　哑婶说，今天中午给我们做红烧肉！

众姑娘　哦！中午有红烧肉吃了！（众人下）

章兰兰　（内唱）踏遍林场取土样，

一览群山情飞扬。

Meihua　Caixia, we are very serious when working. We just take it easy when taking a break!

Girls　This is called mixing work with rest!

Caixia　You girls!

Sanchun　What are you still standing there for? Get to work!

Girls　Yes!

(sing) Advance on! Advance on! All work and no play will just make me a dull girl... (laugh and swarm towards the steps)

[Yashen enters the stage carrying a bag of rice on her back with a basket of dishes in her hand and looks somewhat tired.

Caixia　Yashen, let me carry it for you! (want to remove the rice from Yashen's back)

Girls　Me, me, me!

Yashen　Ah, ah oh... (make gestures meaning that she can carry it and point at the fresh meat in the basket to show that they can have a good meal[10])

Caixia　Yashen says she'll make braised pork with brown sauce for us at noon!

Girls　Oh! We can have braised pork with brown sauce at noon! (They go offstage)

Zhang Lanlan　(sing inside) Sampling the soils through the farm,
The overall view excites me.

谢主任　兰兰！

章兰兰　谢主任，你说的是什么好消息？

谢主任　林场申请的政府贴息贷款二十万批下来了，镇长通知你去办手续。

章兰兰　谢主任，怎么这么快啊？

谢主任　哎！这说明各级领导都在关心你啊。哦，这里还有一张表，你给填一下。兰兰哪！好好干，有什么问题，及时向我汇报！我走了啊！

章兰兰　谢主任，慢走！

谢主任　你爷爷给你的茶叶蛋别忘了！我走了啊！

章兰兰　你也拿几个吧！

谢主任　好好好……哎呀，真香！

章兰兰　太好了！

（接唱）登高更觉天地宽，

大学毕业回山乡。

圆我心中蓝蓝的梦，

选中山场办林场。

Director Xie　Lanlan!

Zhang Lanlan　Director Xie! What's the good news you're talking about?

Director Xie　The government loan of 200, 000 yuan with a discounted interest rate applied by the tree farm has been approved! The town mayor is asking you to go through the formalities.

Zhang Lanlan　Director Xie, how is it so fast?

Director Xie　Well, this shows that leaders of all levels support you. Oh, here is a form you need to fill it out. Lanlan, do a good job! If there is any problem, report it to me in time! I'm leaving now!

Zhang Lanlan　Director Xie, good bye!

Director Xie　Don't forget the tea eggs your grandpa left you! I'm leaving now!

Zhang Lanlan　Take a few eggs, please.

Director Xie　All right! Ah, it smells good!

Zhang Lanlan　It's great!

(continue to sing)

Ascending makes the world wider.

After graduation I return to

My hometown to realize my dream

Of setting up a tree farm.

南坡种下万竿竹，

要让荒山披绿装。

北坡栽下千亩茶，

五里山冲飘茶香。

再建温室育新苗，

培土嫁接防寒霜。

虽说起步创业难，

幸有天马好同行。

老师同学寄厚望，

知难而进不彷徨！

（白）美女们，快来吃茶叶蛋咯！

[内应："哎，来着！"章兰兰提茶叶蛋下。

[章五姑穿着时髦性感的服装，举着遮阳伞上。

章五姑　太好着，太好着，太好着！

（唱）喏喱水，头上洒，

The south slope will have bamboos
To make the bare mountain green.
The north slope will have tea trees
And the air will smell fragrant.
And I'll build a greenhouse to
Protect seedlings from the cold.
Though it's hard for me to start,
I'm lucky enough to have Tianma.
The expectations from teachers
And classmates give me courage!

(speak) Beauties, come to have tea eggs!

[Voice-over: "Hey, coming!" Zhang Lanlan goes offstage carrying the tea eggs.

[Zhang Wugu enters the stage in fashionable and sexy clothes, holding a sunshade.

Zhang Wugu Wonderful! Wonderful! Wonderful!

(sing) The gel water on my hair

嫩面霜,脸上搽。

徐娘半老风韵在,

青山村里一枝花。

(说唱)挣钱全凭一张嘴,

说得秃头长黑发。

说得公鸡能下蛋,

(唱)舌翻莲花鹅变鸭。

鹅变鸭!

(白)咦,到着!巧珍,巧珍……你快点出来呀!

[巧珍上。

巧　珍　五姑……

章五姑　(热情)巧珍,我跟你说的事情想好了没有哇?

巧　珍　五姑,说心里话,我不想跟你出去。

章五姑　巧珍,你真愿意在这破场子里干?

巧　珍　我觉得兰兰有理想,有能力,对我们像亲姐妹,这个林场一定办得好!

And the cream on my face
Keep my charm though I'm not young.
I'm a beauty in the village.
(rap) I earn money all by talking,
Even the bald man can grow hair
And the rooster can lay eggs.
(sing) I'm skillful to turn a goose
Into a duck!
(speak) Oh, here am I! Qiaozhen, Qiaozhen, come out quickly!

[Qiaozhen enters the stage.

Qiaozhen   Wugu...

Zhang Wugu   (enthusiastic) Qiaozhen, have you made a decision about what I told you?

Qiaozhen   Wugu, to be honest, I don't want to go out with you.

Zhang Wugu   Qiaozhen, do you really want to work in this shabby farm?

Qiaozhen   I think Lanlan is ambitious and capable and treats us like her own sisters. This tree farm is sure to succeed!

章五姑　就算她章兰兰把这个林场办成国际一流，大钱还不是她赚了。你，一个小员工，还不是拿点血汗钱。巧珍，来来来，坐坐坐，不如趁现在年轻漂亮，去挣大钱！搞这点小钱不值！

巧　珍　跟你就能挣大钱？

章五姑　保底数，每月五千。运气好的话，一天就能挣五千。

巧　珍　你越说我越不敢相信了。

章五姑　你不信啊？（亮手指上的钻戒）你看，这枚钻戒，半克拉，五万！巧珍，跟五姑后面，吃的是智力饭，挣的是轻巧钱！巧珍，听我讲，跟着我就有钱途，就有财路。要成功，先发疯，头脑简单向前冲！摇身一变就是大老板。

巧　珍　五姑，这不是做传销啊？这样的事情不光彩，我不干。

章五姑　什么光彩不光彩呀？现在是笑贫不笑娼，挣到钱就光彩！（火）巧珍，告诉你，这个月工资我已经付过了。你妈妈已经拿了我五千块。

巧　珍　我妈妈知道是出去干这种事吗？（脱下衣帽扔给章五姑）

Zhang Wugu	Even if Zhang Lanlan makes this tree farm a first-class business in the world, it will be she who earns the big money yet. You, just an employee of the tree farm, will still make the hard-earned money. Qiaozhen, come to sit here. It's better to make a fortune while you are young and beautiful! It's not worthwhile to earn so little money!
Qiaozhen	I can make a fortune by following you?
Zhang Wugu	At least 5,000 yuan every month. If luckier, you can earn 5,000 yuan a day.
Qiaozhen	The more you talk, the less I believe you.
Zhang Wugu	You don't believe me? (show her the diamond ring) Look! This diamond ring is half a carat, and it's worth 50,000 yuan. Qiaozhen, following me, you can earn easy money with intelligence! Qiaozhen, listen to me. If you follow me, you will have the goose that lays the golden eggs. To succeed, go crazy first, head forward with a simple mind! You will turn into a big boss.
Qiaozhen	Wugu, isn't this a pyramid scheme? It's not honorable to do such a thing. I won't do it.
Zhang Wugu	What is honorable or dishonorable? Now people are "not laughing at the prostitution but the poverty". If you can earn money, you'll be honorable! (angrily) Qiaozhen, let me tell you this. I have already paid your salary for this month. Your mother took 5,000 yuan from me.
Qiaozhen	Does my mother know that I'm going out to do this? (take off the coat and hat and throw them to Zhang Wugu)

［章兰兰、彩霞上。

章五姑　巧珍，不干也可以，算你违约，违约就得翻倍赔钱。一万块，拿出来！

章兰兰　章五姑，巧珍跟你签了什么合约哇？

章五姑　哟，大场长，这是我和巧珍之间的事，与你们林场不相干。

巧　珍　场长，她要我去做传销，去骗钱！

章兰兰　章五姑，这是违法知不知道！你去骗钱还要拉巧珍下水[11]，她现在是林场员工，我要对她负责！

章五姑　章兰兰，五姑可是吃盐长大的[12]，吓唬谁呀！我就是违法你管得着吗？巧珍，巧珍哪，你们家太穷了，我一看你妈妈病成那个样子，我的心都痛哦！我是给你们家扶贫哪！

巧　珍（犹豫）这……

彩　霞　巧珍，你千万不能犯糊涂，回去！

章兰兰　巧珍，你真要走吗？

章五姑　过了这个村，就没有那个店[13]。走吧！

［巧珍看了看章兰兰，欲随章五姑下。

[Zhang Lanlan and Caixia enter the stage.

Zhang Wugu   Qiaozhen, if you don't want to do that, you are breaking the contract. Then you'll have to pay twice. Ten thousand yuan. Now pay me!

Zhang Lanlan   Zhang Wugu, what contract did Qiaozhen sign with you?

Zhang Wugu   Oops, dear director, this is a matter between Qiaozhen and me. It has nothing to do with your tree farm.

Qiaozhen   Director, she asks me to do pyramid selling and cheat others out of money!

Zhang Lanlan   Zhang Wugu, don't you know you're breaking the law! You're scamming others and even try to coerce Qiaozhen to do that with you[11]. Now she is an employee of my tree farm, I'm responsible for her.

Zhang Wugu   Zhang Lanlan, I have experienced a lot of things[12]. Who are you trying to scare? Even if I break the law, is it your business? Qiaozhen, Qiaozhen, your family is too poor. How my heart hurts when I see your mother is suffering from illness! I'm helping your family out of poverty.

Qiaozhen   (hesitant) Well...

Caixia   Qiaozhen, do the right thing. Go back!

Zhang Lanlan   Qiaozhen, do you really want to go?

Zhang Wugu   If you miss the chance, you won't have it again[13]. Let's go!

[Looking at Zhang Lanlan, Qiaozhen intends to go offstage following Zhang Wugu.

巧　珍　兰兰姐，家里太穷了，我想出去看看！

章五姑　这就对着！（搂住巧珍）走吧！（对着章兰兰、彩霞）咕噜拜！哈哈哈！（二人下）

章兰兰　（看着巧珍离去，气恼心烦）咳！

（唱）刚刚起步就受挫折，

这真是事非经过不知难！

有道是不做和尚头不冷[14]，

彩　霞　（唱）巧珍离去就怕人心散！

章兰兰　我就担心巧珍会上当！

彩　霞　这个章五姑，三天两头就来林场生事，搅得人心不安。

章兰兰　（心烦意乱）烦人，真烦人哪！

彩　霞　兰兰，你想打退堂鼓[15]？

章兰兰　我已经骑在老虎背上下不来了！彩霞，你可要陪着我！

彩　霞　兰兰，我有多大能耐？你最好找一个志同道合的合作伙伴，与你一起来办林场。

Qiaozhen Sister Lanlan, my family is too poor, so I want to go out to have a try.

Zhang Wugu That's right! (put her arm around Qiaozhen) Just go with me! (to Zhang Lanlan and Caixia) Good bye! Hahaha. (The two go offstage)

Zhang Lanlan (Watching Qiaozhen leave, annoyed and upset) Alas!

(sing) From the beginning frustration,

I know it's really hard to go through it.

It's said that a monk knows his head is cold,[14]

Caixia (sing) I'm afraid Qiaozhen's leaving disheartens them.

Zhang Lanlan I'm worried that Qiaozhen will be fooled.

Caixia Zhang Wugu comes to our tree farm to make trouble every two or three days, and makes people feel uneasy.

Zhang Lanlan (annoyed and perplexed) Annoying! Really annoying!

Caixia Lanlan, are you beating a retreat[15]?

Zhang Lanlan I'm now in a dilemma as if I'm riding a tiger and cannot get off it. Caixia, you have to stay with me!

Caixia Lanlan, how much know-how do I have? You'd better find a like-minded partner to run this tree farm with you.

章兰兰　我也这么想,可理想人选难找哇!

彩　霞　你的网友天马怎么样?

章兰兰　天马?(惊)鬼丫头,你偷看我的QQ了吧?

彩　霞　做贼心虚了吧?我不会偷看你的QQ。你不是说林场规划图纸是天马帮你做的吗?这个天马是个男的吧?

章兰兰　可能是。我们还没有见过面呢!

彩　霞　兰兰,你好像对天马有那么一点意思。

章兰兰　也许有吧。我就怕他长得像个外星人,小脑袋,长脖子……(手机响,接听)喂,谁呀?

[周立凡的声音:"芳草,我是天马。"

章兰兰　(意外)天马,你怎么知道我的手机号码?

[周立凡的声音:"信息时代,这还不容易吗?"

章兰兰　你,你还没有得到我的同意呀!

[周立凡声音:"我会向你道歉!明天早上,请到青山村桥头路口接我,一定!"

章兰兰　天马,你不要来!喂,喂……

Zhang Lanlan　I also think so, but it's hard to find an ideal one!

Caixia　What about your online friend, Tianma?

Zhang Lanlan　Tianma? (astonished) Smart girl, you peeped at my QQ?

Caixia　Is something going on? I didn't peep at your QQ. Didn't you say it was Tianma who helped you make the planning drawings of the tree farm? Is this Tianma a he?

Zhang Lanlan　Maybe. We haven't met yet!

Caixia　Lanlan, you seem to have a little interest in Tianma.

Zhang Lanlan　Maybe. But I'm afraid that he looks like an alien with a small head and a long neck! (Her cell phone rings and she answers) Hello, who is that?

[Zhou Lifan's voice-over: "Fangcao, this is Tianma."

Zhang Lanlan　(surprised) Tianma, how do you know my cell phone number?

[Zhou Lifan's voice-over: "Isn't this so easy in the information age?"

Zhang Lanlan　You haven't got my consent yet!

[Zhou Lifan's voice-over: "I will apologize to you later on. Tomorrow morning, please pick me up at the bridge in Qingshan Village."

Zhang Lanlan　Tianma, don't come here! Hello, hello...

彩　霞　人家关机了！芳草姑娘，明天就来一出“兰桥会”[16]吧！

章兰兰　什么兰桥会？这个天马，不是强人所难吗？

彩　霞　兰兰姐……（附耳）

章兰兰　你这个小怪妹！

[切光。

Caixia	He turned off his cell phone. Fangcao, have a Lanqiao Bridge date[16] tomorrow!
Zhang Lanlan	What Lanqiao Bridge date? Isn't Tianma forcing me to meet him?
Caixia	Sister Lanlan... (Caixia whispers to Lanlan)
Zhang Lanlan	You little quirky girl!

[Light switches.

第二场

［青山村桥头路口

［汽车鸣笛开走的声音。周立凡内声:"师傅,再见!"

［周立凡身着休闲服,拖着一只高档旅行箱上。他如同出笼之鸟,神采飞扬。

周立凡　（登高大喊）芳草,我来啦！我来啦！

（唱）悄悄离家寻芳草,

心旷神怡步履矫。

虽然是,山环水复陌生地,

就如同,梦里来过千百遭。

离家如同出笼鸟,

心如春潮逐浪高。

本以为与芳草相距甚远,

却原来半日行程即可到。

Act Ⅱ

[At the end of the bridge in Qingshan Village.

[The honking of a car is leaving away. Zhou Lifan's voice-over: "Sir, Goodbye!"

[Zhou Lifan enters the stage in casual clothes, lugging an exclusive suitcase. He is in high spirit like a bird out of a cage.

Zhou Lifan (ascend a height yelling) Fangcao, I'm here! I'm here!

(sing) I left home to find Fangcao,
Quietly, happily and swiftly.
Though it's a strange place with mountains and rivers,
It seems I've been here many times in my dream.
Like a bird out of a cage,
I'm leaving home excitedly.
I thought that it was far away from Fangcao,
but in fact, it was just a half-day trip.

几天来辗转反侧难安睡，

一颗心早已飞到青山坳。

芳草啊，莫要怨我太急躁，

岁月如歌处处涌动创业潮！

是绿色的事业在呼唤我，

芳草呀，让我们携手来把重担挑！

彩　霞　喂！你是天马吗？

周立凡　（急切迎上）你是芳草？

［二人对视，观察。

彩　霞　（旁白）兰兰还真有眼力！他与兰兰真是天生的一对！

周立凡　（旁白）她不像我心中的芳草！

周立凡　芳草，你的声音好像变了！

彩　霞　声音经过信号传输，多少会有点失真的。

周立凡　芳草，你不会责怪我吧？这么急切地前来见你！

彩　霞　不，你早就该来了。兰兰她办那么大的林场，一个人累得够呛！

I've been tossing and turning for a few days,
My mind has already flown to Qingshan Col.
Fangcao, don't blame me for my impatience,
Tides of starting business surge everywhere in the years!
It's the green business that is calling me,
Fangcao, let's join hands together to carry the heavy burden!

Caixia Hello, are you Tianma?

Zhou Lifan (go up eagerly) Are you Fangcao?

[They look each other in the eye, watching.

Caixia (speak aside) Lanlan really has good taste! He and Lanlan are a natural couple!

Zhou Lifan (speak aside) She isn't my Fangcao!

Zhou Lifan Fangcao, your voice seems to have changed!

Caixia Sound is somewhat distorted when transmitted as a signal.

Zhou Lifan Fangcao, you won't blame me for coming to see you so eagerly, will you?

Caixia No, you should have come earlier. Lanlan almost works herself to death running such a large tree farm alone!

周立凡　兰兰？她是谁呀？

彩　霞　就是芳草哇！

周立凡　那你是——

彩　霞　（扑哧一笑）嘻嘻，我叫彩霞，是章兰兰场长的面试官。只有过了我这一关，你们才可以见面。

周立凡　啊！她人在哪儿？

彩　霞　急什么，面试还没有完呢！天马，你的真名叫什么？

周立凡　周立凡。

彩　霞　有证件吗？

周立凡　还要证件？（气）这是身份证！（掏出身份证）

彩　霞　（拿过身份证仔细看了看）周立凡！

周立凡　（不悦，拿回身份证）这个芳草呀，也太不相信人了！或许我不该来！（拖起旅行箱往回走）

彩　霞　（急拦）哎！

［章兰兰已经在场，她走过来。

章兰兰　天马！

Zhou Lifan　Lanlan? Who is she?

Caixia　She is Fangcao!

Zhou Lifan　Then you are...

Caixia　(burst into a laugh) Hee hee! I'm Caixia, the interviewer working for Zhang Lanlan, the director of the tree farm. You can only meet after you pass my interview.

Zhou Lifan　Oh! Where is she?

Caixia　Take it easy! The interview isn't over yet. Tianma, what's your real name?

Zhou Lifan　Zhou Lifan.

Caixia　Got any certificate?

Zhou Lifan　Any certificate? (angry) This is the ID card! (take out the ID card)

Caixia　(take the ID card and look at it carefully) Zhou Lifan!

Zhou Lifan　(unhappily take back the ID card) Fangcao is too cautious to trust me! Maybe I shouldn't have come here. (haul his suitcase and head back)

Caixia　(stop him immediately) Hey!

[Zhang Lanlan is already present and comes over.

Zhang Lanlan　Tianma!

［周立凡听到章兰兰声音，马上立住。

章兰兰　天马，是我多了一个心眼，对不起。

彩　霞　报告芳草同志，面试工作完成了！（小声）九十九点九九分，合格！下面的戏该你唱了，我去通知哑婶摆酒接风！（朝章兰兰做个鬼脸后笑着下）

章兰兰　天马，你还在生气吗？

周立凡　我们相识已久，网上无话不谈，你却还搞什么面试，多难堪哪！

章兰兰　天马，虚拟世界给人们的教训太多了。

周立凡　我在网上对你说过一句假话吗？

章兰兰　我毕竟是女孩子，怕受到伤害。你，你就不能理解吗？

周立凡　理解？

章兰兰　（嗔怒）天马，我向你道歉还不行吗？

周立凡　芳草，不，现在应该喊你章兰兰！

周立凡　兰兰，我早就盼着这一天哪！

（唱）几天来一直难安寝，

[Zhou Lifan immediately stands still when he hears Zhang Lanlan's voice.

Zhang Lanlan Tianma, it's me who thinks too much. I'm sorry.

Caixia Reporting to Comrade Fangcao! The interview is finished! (speak in a low voice) He scores ninety-nine point ninety-nine! Qualified! Now is your turn. I will ask Yashen to prepare a welcoming dinner for him. (she makes a face to Lanlan and goes off the stage laughing)

Zhang Lanlan Tianma, are you still angry with me?

Zhou Lifan We have known each other for a long time and talked about everything online, but you make me interviewed! How embarrassed I am!

Zhang Lanlan Tianma, the virtual world has taught people too much.

Zhou Lifan: Did I ever tell you a lie online?

Zhang Lanlan After all, I'm a girl and afraid of being hurt. Can't you, can't you understand?

Zhou Lifan Understand?

Zhang Lanlan (angry) Tianma, I apologize to you, ok?

Zhou Lifan Fangcao, oh no, now I should call you Zhang Lanlan!

Zhou Lifan Lanlan, I've been looking forward to this day since long ago!

(sing) I haven't slept well for a few days

思绪早已飞到青山村。

身不由己跟着感觉走，

相见如同在梦境。

兰兰你或许不相信

（插白）兰兰，我凭想象给你画了一幅模拟画像，

（接唱）不像十分像九分！

章兰兰　没想到你还有画画的才能！

周立凡　当初人家都叫我画家。

章兰兰　画家？

周立凡　不过前面要加上业余两个字！

章兰兰　业余画家也不错啊，难怪你的设计图画得那么漂亮。

周立凡　过奖了！兰兰，请看！

章兰兰　像，太像了！

周立凡　我就说嘛！不像十分像九分！

章兰兰　你都把我画成老太婆啦！

Because my thoughts have already been here.
I can't help following my feelings
As if we meet in my dream.
Lanlan, you may not believe that

(speak) Lanlan, I drew you a simulated portrait according to my imagination.

(continue to sing) It's almost the same as you!

Zhang Lanlan　I have never thought you can paint!

Zhou Lifan　Originally people called me painter.

Zhang Lanlan　Painter?

Zhou Lifan　However, the word amateur must be added to the word!

Zhang Lanlan　It's also good to be an amateur painter. No wonder your design drawings are so beautiful.

Zhou Lifan　I'm flattered! Lanlan, look at it, please!

Zhang Lanlan　Same, almost the same!

Zhou Lifan　I told you so! It's almost the same as you!

Zhang Lanlan　You painted me almost like an old woman!

周立凡　啊呀！坏着，这是给我奶奶画的，这一张肯定不会错，兰兰，你看像不像？

章兰兰　不，不像，这不是我！

（唱）像上的女孩太靓丽，
风情万种像明星。
妩媚冷艳骄矜样，
兰兰我自知之明逊三分。
既有你心中偶像在，
快去追寻你意中人。（将模拟画像递还）

周立凡　兰兰！

（唱）你就是我意中人，
你比画像更精神。
既然来到你身边，
上天入地把你跟！

章兰兰　立凡！

（唱）我看你书生意气十分浓，

Zhou Lifan Sorry, sorry, this is for my granny. This is the right one! Lanlan, look, does it look alike?

Zhang Lanlan No, not at all. This is not me!

(sing) The girl you drew is too pretty,

As alluring as a star,

Charming, cold and arrogant.

I know I can't compare myself with her.

Since this is your idol in your mind,

Hurry to find the lady of your heart.

(give back the simulated portrait to him)

Zhou Lifan Lanlan!

(sing) You're the lady of my heart and

Look livelier than the portrait.

Since I come to you, I will

Follow you wherever you go!

Zhang Lanlan Lifan!

(sing) You are still so bookish in my opinion.

在家里定然是乖乖宝宝小亲亲。
兰兰我不留城市做白领，
愿与青山伴晨昏。
林场建设刚起步，
面临困难与艰辛。
兰兰吃苦有准备，
实现蓝图非几春！
一时热情难持久，
莫为兰兰误前程！

周立凡　兰兰！
（唱）前程要靠自己创，
认准目标向前奔！
你为绿色洒汗水，
我为绿色献青春。
让荒山披上一层绿，
鸟语花香四季春。

You must be the obedient baby and little dear at home.
I choose not to be a city white collar
But to set up the tree farm.
It has just started building
With difficulties and hardship.
I'm ready to bear the hard years
Of realizing the blueprint!
For your passion can't last long,
Don't miss your future for me!

Zhou Lifan Lanlan!

(sing) One should create his own future
And move forward to his goal.
Just like you sweat for the green,
I'll devote my youth to it!
Let's turn the barren mountains green,
Make it spring-like all the year.

莫道书生空议论，
创业成材在基层。
志同道合手挽手，
高山流水结知音。
十年树木育栋梁，
让我们携手创业奔前程！

(白) 兰兰，坐。兰兰，我的导师说，绿色产业是关系到人类未来的伟大产业。他支持我，鼓励我把最新的科技成果应用起来。他还说要把金凤林场当作他的科研基地呢！万事开头难，我有思想准备。

章兰兰　立凡，来！

[章兰兰与周立凡慢慢抬起手，两只手紧紧握住。

二　人　(合唱)二人牵起手，
连起两颗心。
举眉互凝视，
心灵早相通。

章兰兰　天马，我想问你一个问题。

周立凡　问吧。

Don't think it's a scholar's empty talk,
Success starts from the grassroots.
We're so like-minded to be
The appreciative bosom friends.
Trees of ten years breed pillars.
Let's start our business together for future!

(speak) Lanlan, sit. Lanlan, my supervisor said that the green industry is a great industry and concerns the future of humanity. He supported me and encouraged me to apply the latest scientific and technological achievements. He also said that he would make Jinfeng Tree Farm his research base! I know that everything is difficult at the beginning. I'm mentally prepared for it.

Zhang Lanlan　Lifan, come with me!

[Zhang Lanlan and Zhou Lifan slowly raise up their hands and hold firmly.]

The Two　(chorus) Hand in hand they are,
Two hearts are combined.
Eyes to eyes they fix,
Soul to soul they've been.

Zhang Lanlan　Tianma, I've meant to ask you a question.

Zhou Lifan　OK.

章兰兰　你父母支持你这样做吗？

周立凡　反对，一百个反对！

章兰兰　当然，父母都希望自己的孩子生活得幸福！

周立凡　兰兰，什么是幸福？就是从事自己所热爱的事业，和自己喜欢的人在一起！

章兰兰　还是让时间来检验我们吧！立凡，走，到林场去。

周立凡　场长同志，有睡觉的地方吗？

章兰兰　有。不过，肯定没有你家里好，有点像诸葛草庐。[17]

周立凡　体验一下原生态的生活，不是很有诗意吗？

［章五姑上，看见他俩，躲闪至一旁。

章兰兰　来，把箱子给我。（拉动旅行箱）

周立凡　我来！

章兰兰　还是给我吧！哟，很沉嘛！

周立凡　我这箱子可是百宝箱，有电脑、资料、人民币，还有……

章兰兰　还有什么？不会是摇头丸吧？

周立凡　暂时保密。就像你没有把为什么爱上林业的秘密告诉我一样！

Zhang Lanlan Do your parents support you to do so?

Zhou Lifan They don't.

Zhang Lanlan Of course, parents always want their children to live a happy life!

Zhou Lifan Lanlan, what is happiness? It is doing what you love and being with the person you love!

Zhang Lanlan Let's see how it'll work out for us! Lifan, come on, go to the tree farm.

Zhou Lifan Comrade director, is there a place for me to sleep?

Zhang Lanlan Of course, there is. But it's not as good as your home, a bit like the thatched cottage of the mastermind Zhuge Liang.[17]

Zhou Lifan Isn't it poetic to experience the original ecological life?

[Zhang Wugu goes onstage. She dodges aside when seeing them.

Zhang Lanlan Well, give me the suitcase. (pull the suitcase)

Zhou Lifan Let me take it.

Zhang Lanlan Just give it to me! Oh, it's heavy!

Zhou Lifan This is my treasure chest with my laptop, materials, RMB, and...

Zhang Lanlan And what else? It's not ecstasy, is it?

Zhou Lifan Let's keep it a secret for the time being. Just like you haven't told me why as a girl you fall in love with forestry!

章兰兰　留点悬念也好。跟我走吧！

[章兰兰拉着旅行箱和周立凡有说有笑地下。

章五姑　(见他俩去远，诡谲一笑)啊嗟，章兰兰这个小妖精还真是个货色[18]呢！水不惊，鱼不跳[19]就勾来一个帅哥！这小子定是色迷了心窍，好日子不过，跑到这山里来吃腌菜臭萝卜！哪家的儿子算是瞎养啰！

二顺子　哪个讲我这个儿子瞎养着？看见着吧，这是我在山沟里摸的几条小鱼，回去给我爸做下酒菜。

章五姑　啊哟，哪个不知道你二顺子勤劳发狠，又自食其力，孝顺你爸又孝顺你妈。

二顺子　所以我叫二顺子嘛！

章五姑　我刚才讲的不是你哦！

二顺子　那你讲的是哪一个？

章五姑　哪家的帅小伙被章兰兰勾上山来着！

二顺子　该死！我二顺子又多了个竞争对手！

Zhang Lanlan It's good to have some suspense. Follow me!

[Pulling the suitcase, Zhang Lanlan goes offstage with Zhou Lifan, talking and laughing.

Zhang Wugu (seeing them go far away, she smiles slyly) Oho, Zhang Lanlan, this goblin, is a real someone![18] She seduced a handsome man without any fuss![19] This bloke must have been obsessed with her beauty! So, he doesn't want the good days but the hard days in the mountains! Oho! Whose son is this youth? He is raised for nothing.

Ershunzi Who says that I'm raised for nothing as the son? You see these small fish I caught in the gully? These are the dish for my dad to drink!

Zhang Wugu Oh, nobody doesn't know that you are hardworking and self-reliant, filial to both your father and mother.

Ershunzi So, my name is Ershunzi!

Zhang Wugu It's not you who I was talking about just now!

Ershunzi Then who is it?

Zhang Wugu It's the unknown handsome youth seduced by Zhang Lanlan to the mountain!

Ershunzi Damn it! I have another competitor!

章五姑　什么竞争对手,依我看你二顺子就是吃亏在打扮上!你要是休闲西装一穿,小包一夹,不晓得有多神气哦!

二顺子　可是的?

章五姑　是的嘛!

二顺子　那我找我老爸要钱,明天就去镇上买!

章五姑　那到时候就 O 了 K 了!

二顺子　五姑啊,你今天又到山上来做么事啊?

章五姑　啊哟,昨天下山出大事了!

二顺子　么事啊?你快讲啊!

章五姑　昨天下山的时候,我钻戒上的一块玻璃掉着!

二顺子　五姑,这钻戒上的玻璃怎么讲啊?

章五姑　你快帮五姑找找,找到着有奖励!

二顺子　奖励多少钱?

章五姑　五块钱。

二顺子　啊哟!一瓶饮料的钱!

章五姑　好好好,我再加五块,十块钱!

Zhang Wugu	What competitor? In my eyes, you are at a disadvantage in how you dress! If you wear a leisure suit and carry a small bag under your arm, you don't know how smart you will look!
Ershunzi	Is that true?
Zhang Wugu	Of course, yes.
Ershunzi	OK, I will ask my dad for money and go to town tomorrow!
Zhang Wugu	Then it will be OK!
Ershunzi	Wugu, for what do you come to the mountain again today?
Zhang Wugu	Oho, something big happened yesterday when I was going down the mountain!
Ershunzi	What's that? Tell me quickly!
Zhang Wugu	Yesterday when I was going down the mountain, a piece of glass fell out of my diamond ring!
Ershunzi	Wugu, what do you mean by *glass* on your *diamond* ring?
Zhang Wugu	Just help me to find it. I will reward you for that!
Ershunzi	How much is the reward?
Zhang Wugu	Five yuan!
Ershunzi	Whoa! Only enough for a soda!
Zhang Wugu	Well, well, I'll give you five yuan more, ten yuan!

二顺子　照嘛！

章五姑　快找，快找找……

[切光。

Ershunzi　　OK!

Zhang Wugu　　Quick! Quick! Find it, find it...

[Light switches.

第三场

[嬉子湖畔。

[陈设讲究的客厅。对称的两扇门通向左右两间卧室。

[周志豪在打电话。

周志豪 （唱）半生辛苦为发家，

养鱼养蟹养王八。

改革开放政策好，

办起公司把财发。

生意兴隆事事顺，

谁料家里尽出茬！

养个儿子不听话，

任性而为我没有办法。

不辞而别离家走，

好日子被搅成一团乱麻[20]！

Act Ⅲ

[The lakeside of Xizi Lake.

[A well-furnished living room. Two symmetrical doors respectively lead to bedrooms on the left and right.

[Zhou Zhihao is making a call.

Zhou Zhihao (sing) I've worked hard for half a life
And got rich by aquafarming.
The good policy of reform
Allows me to make a fortune.
Business and everything go well,
But who expects troubles at home!
My disobedient son is so
Willful that I don't know what to do.
He left home with no message,
So, my good days have been turned into a mess[20]!

[电话铃响。周志豪接电话:"谁呀?"

[话筒里男人的声音:"哥,是我,立凡回来了吗?"

周志豪　该找的地方全找了,寻人启事也播了,一点儿消息也没有!

[话筒里的声音:"哥,别急。他又不是小伢子,会回来的。"

周志豪　不回来,除非死在外面!(搁下电话)

[刘惠芹神情憔悴地从内房跑出。

刘惠芹　死在外面!志豪,谁死啦?你说,谁死啦?

周志豪　谁死了?我要被这个小杂种气死了!

刘惠芹　你骂谁是小杂种?

周志豪　还有哪个,你那个宝贝儿子!

刘惠芹　儿子都被你逼走了,你还骂他,你的心好狠啰!

(唱)儿子毕业回家来,

成了你的出气胎[21],

横挑鼻子竖挑眼[22],

他在家中无法呆!

[The phone rings. Zhou Zhihao answers the phone: "Hello, who is that?"

[A man's voice comes from the receiver: "Hello, bro, it's me. Is Lifan back?"

Zhou Zhihao　I've sought all the places I should look for, and broadcasted a notice for missing persons. There is no news at all!

[The voice from the receiver: "Bro, don't worry. He is not a tot. He'll be back."

Zhou Zhihao　He won't be back unless he dies outside! (put the phone down)

[Liu Huiqin runs out of the inner room with a haggard look.

Liu Huiqin　Dies outside! Zhihao, who died? Tell me, who died?

Zhou Zhihao　Who died? I'm to be infuriated to death by this little bastard!

Liu Huiqin　Who are you scolding as a bastard?

Zhou Zhihao　Who else, your dear son!

Liu Huiqin　He has already been forced away by you, but you still scold him. How cruelhearted you are!

(sing) Since he came home after graduation,
He has become your punching bag[21].
You pick his faults right and left [22]
So that he can't stay at home!

不把立凡找回来，

我要与你两拆开！

周志豪　拆开、拆开……

刘惠芹　（哭）你……立凡，儿子，你在哪里哟？

周志豪　（烦）儿子离家，都是我的错吗？叫他参加招聘，不去！叫他去考公务员，不去！叫他到我公司上班，理都不理！整天躲在屋里玩电脑、上网。连吃饭也要三催四请，你说这还像话吗？就不该让他念这个大学！像他妹妹，念个大专，跟在我后面，钱也挣了，说不定老婆也娶了。真是身在福中不知福！

刘惠芹　儿子才多大呀？他享你什么福啦？

周志豪　二十多岁还小哇？我像他这样大早就养家糊口了，我吃了多少苦哇！

刘惠芹　那是你命不好，生不逢时，活该！

周志豪　真是惯子不孝，肥田出瘪稻[23]，都是被你惯的！

刘惠芹　你……

If you don't find Lifan back,

I'm going to break up with you!

Zhou Zhihao Break up... Break up...

Liu Huiqin (crying) You... Lifan, my son, where are you?

Zhou Zhihao (annoyed) Is it all my fault that he left home? I asked him to find a job, but he refused! I asked him to take the civil service examination, he refused again! I asked him to work for me, he simply ignored me! He just spends all day in his room being with his computer and surfing the Internet. We even had to urge him two or three times for meals. Do you think it is reasonable? He shouldn't have been allowed to go to college. If he had been like his sister, working for me and earning money, maybe now he would have married. He really takes everything for granted!

Liu Huiqin How old is he? What does he take for granted?

Zhou Zhihao Is he still young in his twenties? I started to support my family at his age. How much I have suffered!

Liu Huiqin That is due to your bad fate for you were born in a wrong time. You deserve it!

Zhou Zhihao The spoiled child is not filial, just as the fertile field comes out with the withered rice[23]. It's you who spoils him!

Liu Huiqin You...

周志豪　你……

[周立娜从另一门内冲出。

周立娜　（烦躁，发火）吵，吵，吵！烦死人了！人跑了能吵回来吗？

哥哥离家出走，你们两个都有责任！

周志豪　我有什么责任？我是打了他还是骂了他？

刘惠芹　立娜，你说，妈妈哪一点对不起他？

周立娜　爸、妈，旁观者清[24]，你们都听我说！

（唱）先说爸爸搞家长制，

财大气粗爱训人。

哥哥的意见全不听，

不讲道理好瞪眼睛。

他的人生你设计，

越俎代庖[25]太过分。

哥哥的人格要尊重，

莫以为只要给予就是亲情。

哥哥他人长树大[26]有思想，

是你的儿子更是社会的公民。

Zhou Zhihao　You...

[Zhou Lina rushes out of another door.

Zhou Lina　(irritable, furious) Quarreling! Quarreling! Quarreling! It's annoying! Can he come back if you keep quarreling after he ran away? You're both responsible for his running away from home!

Zhou Zhihao　What responsibility do I have? Did I hit him or scold him?

Liu Huiqin　Lina, what have I done wrong?

Zhou Lina　Dad, mom, the onlooker sees the game best[24]. You all listen to me!

(sing) Let's start with dad's paternalism.
You're rich and like to teach others,
Fully neglect my brother's suggestions,
Unreasonably like staring at him.
You try to design his life,
But it's too much to meddle[25].
You should respect his character,
Don't think that your one-side giving is family love!
My brother is a grown-up[26] with his own ideas,
A citizen of society as well as your son.

周志豪　我，我是这样吗？（有点触动）

刘惠芹　说得一点都不错！当个土经理，回家也摆个领导架子，说一不二，谁受得了哇！

周志豪　你说，我能领导你吗？

刘惠芹　你……

周立娜　妈，现在该说你啦！

周志豪　立娜，是该好好说说你妈！

周立娜　（唱）妈妈有重男轻女[27]的旧脑筋，

对哥哥溺爱太过分。

含在嘴里怕化掉，

不捧在手上不放心[28]。

好像哥哥没长大，

他永远是个长不大的小学生。

溺爱过分生逆反，

雏鹰长大当凌云！

我的妈妈呀！

Zhou Zhihao Well, am I such a person? (a little convinced)

Liu Huiqin Totally right! Being a countrified boss, you also put on leadership airs when you are home. And you have things your own way. Who can stand it!

Zhou Zhihao Can I boss you around?

Liu Huiqin You...

Zhou Lina Mom, now it's time to talk about you!

Zhou Zhihao Lina, you should talk about your mom!

Zhou Lina (sing) Mom has got the old thought of son preference[27],

So, you dote on my brother too much.

He is the apple of your eye

As well as your beloved son[28].

It seems that brother hasn't grown up

And he will remain a childish student forever.

You never think his rebellion

Starts from your overindulgence!

Do you know it? Mom!

周志豪　立娜，说得对！

刘惠芹　对个鬼！说我重男轻女，我对你哪点差呀？手心手背都是肉[29]！

周立娜　儿子是手心，女儿是手背，是有那么点差别！

刘惠芹　说我溺爱你哥哥是不假，他多争气呀！从小学到大学，从没让我操心。我溺爱他，值！

周志豪　值？哼，他领过你的情吗？还不是一走了之！

刘惠芹　这怪我吗？都是你逼的！

周志豪　我逼过他吗？你胡说八道！

刘惠芹　你胡说！

周志豪　你胡说！

周立娜　不要再吵了，不要再吵了，你们再吵啊，我也离家出走了！

周志豪　（担心）立娜，我们不是着急吗？

周立娜　你们都是瞎着急！哥哥出走是有准备、有目标的。说不定是件好事。不出三五年，准能把你们的媳妇、孙子一起带回家！

Zhou Zhihao	Lina, you're right!
Liu Huiqin	Not right at all! You say I prefer boys to girls, but do I treat you bad? Both the palm and the back of the hand are made of flesh[29].
Zhou Lina	Your son is the palm and your daughter is the back of the hand. Indeed, there is a little difference!
Liu Huiqin	It's true for you to say that I dote on your brother. What a high achiever he is! I never worried about him from primary school to college. He deserves my doting!
Zhou Zhihao	Does he? Hum, did he ever appreciate your doting? Didn't he run away from home!
Liu Huiqin	Is this my fault? It's because you forced him!
Zhou Zhihao	Did I? You talk nonsense!
Liu Huiqin	You do!
Zhou Zhihao	You do!
Zhou Lina	No more quarreling! No more quarreling! If you don't stop, I'll run away from home too!
Zhou Zhihao	(worried) Lina, we're just worried.
Zhou Lina	It's no use! My brother was prepared and purposeful when he left. Maybe it's a good thing. No more than three or five years, he can bring home your daughter-in-law and grandson together!

刘惠芹　三五年？三五天我都受不了啦！

周志豪　立娜，你哥哥出走，跟你商量过？

周立娜　绝对没有！不过据我分析，哥哥是会他的网友去了！

刘惠芹　会网友？这个网友是男的还是女的？

周立娜　可能是个女的！

刘惠芹　啊！那要是碰上个狐狸精[30]，可怎么办哪！

周立娜　妈，你怎么净往坏处想？狐狸精哪都是坏的呀？哥哥这次出门把林业方面的资料全带走了，我估计他这个网友可能也是学林的。要想查清哥哥的下落，你们都得听我的！

周志豪　听你的？好，你说你说。

周立娜　哥哥把电脑也带走了，他肯定会上网的。我给我所有的网友发了帖子，在网上展开人肉搜索[31]，哥哥一上网，准能逮住！

周志豪　对对对，我们还贴了寻人启事，提供线索者一定重谢！

[门铃响。

刘惠芹　立娜，快去！

Liu Huiqin　Three or five years? I can't bear even for three or five days!

Zhou Zhihao　Lina, did your brother discuss his leaving home with you?

Zhou Lina　Absolutely not! Nevertheless, according to my analysis, he left to meet his net friend!

Liu Huiqin　Meeting with his net friend? Is this net friend a he or she?

Zhou Lina　Might be a she!

Liu Huiqin　Ah! What if he meets a foxtrel[30]?

Zhou Lina　Mom, why do you always think of the worst? Are the foxtrels all bad? My brother has taken away all the materials on forestry this time. I guess this net friend of his also majors in forestry. If you want to find out the where abouts of my brother, you all have to listen to me!

Liu Huiqin　Listen to you? OK. Go on. Go on.

Zhou Lina　He also took away his computer, so I'm sure he will surf the Internet. I have sent posts to all my net friends and started cyber manhunt[31]. As long as my brother is online, I'm sure he can be caught!

Zhou Zhihao　Yeah, yeah, yeah! We also have put up a notice for missing persons. Those who provide us clues must be handsomely rewarded!

[The doorbell rings.

Liu Huiqin　Lina, hurry up!

周立娜　阿姨，请进。阿姨，我来介绍一下，他们是周立凡的父母。爸，妈，这位阿姨是来提供哥哥信息的。

刘惠芹　哎呀，你真是我的贵人哪！立娜，快，快给阿姨沏茶。坐，请坐。

周志豪　请问您贵姓[32]？

章五姑　免贵姓章[33]，立早章，大伙儿都喊我章五姑！

周立娜　（递茶）阿姨，请喝茶！

周志豪　五姑，你知道我儿子的线索吗？

刘惠芹　五姑，你看见我儿子了？

章五姑　看你问的，没有见到人，我辛辛苦苦跑到你们家做么事啊？你儿子，穿了一套名牌休闲服，拉着一只绿色的高档旅行箱。

周立娜　我哥哥身高多少？

章五姑　和你爸爸差不多，比他胖一点。

刘惠芹　不错不错，是他！五姑，我儿子现在人在哪儿？

章五姑　人嘛……嘻嘻，我先说一句，你儿子喝了迷魂汤，中了美人计[34]！

Zhou Lina Aunt, come in please. Aunt, let me make an introduction. They are Zhou Lifan's parents. Dad, mom, this aunt comes to provide some information about my brother.

Liu Huiqin Oh, you are really my lucky star! Lina, be quick, make tea for her. Sit down, sit down please!

Zhou Zhihao May I have your noble family name[32], please?

Zhang Wugu My humble family name is Zhang[33]. Everyone calls me Zhang Wugu!

Zhou Lina (pass her a cup of tea) Aunt, have some tea, please!

Zhou Zhihao Wugu, do you know any clues to my son?

Liu Huiqin Wugu, did you see him?

Zhang Wugu Of course. If I didn't see him, why did I take great pains to come to your home? Your son wears designer casual clothes and pulls an exclusive green suitcase.

Zhou Lina What's the height of my brother?

Zhang Wugu About the same height as your father, a bit taller than him.

Liu Huiqin Right, right, it's him! Wugu, where is my son now?

Zhang Wugu Your son... Let me say so first. Your son has taken a magic potion and fallen into the trap of beauty[34]!

刘惠芹　（慌）啊？喝了迷魂汤，中了美人计！这，这可怎么办哪！

周志豪　五姑，我儿子到底在什么地方？你快说呀！

章五姑　在什么地方？你说在什么地方呢？

周立娜　爸……

周志豪　五姑，要多少酬金，开个价。

章五姑　开个价，其实就是信息费。当然儿子比钱重要，给多少呢？嘻嘻，我也不好说。

刘惠芹　五姑，你就开口说吧！

章五姑　我也生儿养女，母子连心嘛。不给钱也行，就算我学雷锋[35]！

周立娜　既然五姑不肯开价，我来报个价，你辛辛苦苦找到我们家，先付你一千元车马费，马上兑现。如果带着我们找到周立凡，再付九千，这个条件能答应吗？

章五姑　一千加九千，比我心理价位还低了点。好，好，成交。不过，你儿子落脚的地方比较偏僻，山高路险，还有那个小女人比鬼还精，依我看……（与周志豪等人低声交谈）

［切光。

Liu Huiqin (panic) Ah? Taken in the magic potion and fallen into the trap of beauty! What, what can we do?

Zhou Zhihao Wugu, where the hell is my son? Tell me!

Zhang Wugu Where? Where do you think he is?

Zhoulina Dad...

Zhou Zhihao Wugu, how much reward do you want? Name your price.

Zhang Wugu Name my price, actually it is the information fee. Of course, your son is more important than your money. How much should I name? Hee hee, I don't know how to say.

Liu Huiqin Wugu, just say it!

Zhang Wugu I also have children, so I know mother and son are closely connected. It's okay not to have any reward, I just learn from Lei Feng[35] to do a good deed!

Zhou Lina Since Wugu is unwilling to name her price, let me make an offer. It's toilful for you to find our home, so I'll first pay you 1,000 yuan as traffic allowance right now. Then, if you can lead us to Zhou Lifan, I'll pay you another 9,000 yuan. Can you agree to this condition?

Zhang Wugu 1,000 yuan and 9,000 yuan, even a little lower than my expectation. Ok, ok, that's a deal. However, the place where your son stays is very isolated, a high mountain and a dangerous road trip away. What's more, that little woman is more cunning than a fox. In my opinion... (she whispers with Zhou Zhihao and his family)

[Light switches.

第四场

[彩霞、爱莲、禾香、三春扛着成捆的苗木上。

众姑娘　（唱）雨后微风透清新，

山花烂漫芳草新。

背着树苗去山坡，

来年撑起一片荫。

彩　霞　姐妹们，咱们歇哈子吧，累死我了！

爱　莲　要是这里有一条路就好了，汽车呼的一下就上来了！

禾　香　听说就是缺少资金，要好几十万呢！

三　春　哎，场长和周立凡天天跑上跑下，忙着搞土壤调查、项目选址，这几天又在测量那条进山的道路，换了别人早就累得趴下了，他们好像一点都不累，你们说这是为什么啊？

[二顺子上，穿一套新买的休闲西装，手中拿着小包。

Act Ⅳ

[Caixia, Ailian, Hexiang and Sanchun go onstage, carrying bundles of seedlings on their shoulders.

Girls (sing) The breeze is fresh after the rain,
With blooming flowers and green grass.
Carry seedlings to the hillside,
Turn it green in the next year.

Caixia Sisters, let's take a break. I'm exhausted!

Ailian We need a road here, a vehicle would go up with a whoosh!

Hexiang I hear that it is due to the lack of funds, which needs hundreds of thousands of yuan!

Sanchung Hey, the director of the farm and Zhou Lifan work day in and day out, busy with soil survey and project site selection. They have been measuring the road into the mountain. Others will find this job exhausting. But they don't seem tired at all. Do you know why?

[Ershunzi goes onstage, wearing a newly bought casual suit with a small bag in his hand.

二顺子　为什么？这叫爱情的力量！小时候，我爷爷教我唱的："我们的爱情有力量，嘿，我们的爱情有力量！"

彩　霞　二顺子，看看你的打扮，真是丑死着！

众　人　丑死着，呃……

爱　莲　哎，我想起来了，谢主任说过，以后不许二顺子往林场跑。二顺子，你赶紧给我走。

众　人　走！

二顺子　哎哎哎，各位美女，我二顺子早就学好了。

众姑娘　早就学好了？

二顺子　上面已经委任我为桐城市龙眠镇青山村的农电工，你们的光明使者。（掏出上岗证）看，看见了吧！你们也该庆贺庆贺吧！

三　春　婆媳守寡——没工夫[36]，哼！

二顺子　爆竹店失火——自己恭贺[37]，吔！各位美女，为了庆贺我荣升农电工，请各位吃糖，吃糖！哦，告诉你们场长，有事吩咐一声，在下一定效劳！

Ershunzi Why? This is the power of love. When I was a child, my grandpa taught me to sing: "Our love is so powerful! Hey! Our love is so powerful!"

Caixia Ershunzi, look at how you dress! It's so ugly!

Girls So ugly! Yuk...

Ailian Hey, I remember that Director Xie said that Ershunzi was not allowed to come to the tree farm. Ershunzi, I need you to go now.

Girls Go!

Ershunzi Hey, hey, hey! Every beauty, I have already learned from good examples.

Girls Have learned from good examples?

Ershunzi The authorities have already appointed me as the agricultural electrician of Qingshan Village, Longmian Town, Tongcheng City. I am your messenger of light. (take out a work license) Look, see it! You should celebrate too!

Sanchun We have no free time[36]. Hum!

Ershunzi Then let me congratulate myself[37]. Oh yeah! Every beauty, in order to celebrate my promotion to the agricultural electrician, please have some sweets, have some sweets! Oh, tell your director of the farm that if she wants anything done, just tell me. I will be definitely at her service!

[章七爷内喊:“姑娘们!”

众　人　七爷来着!

二顺子　七爷来着!(二顺子闻声,拔腿就跑)

彩　霞　七爷,你今天怎么拎着许多菜上山啊?

章七爷　村里来了两位企业家,说是要在山上搞投资。谢主任正在接待她们,要我带点菜来,过一会她们要上山看看,就留她们在山上吃顿饭。

三　春　场长修路正缺钱呢,投资是好事啊。

章七爷　我就不上去了,你们帮我把菜带上去吧。

众　人　好,来!我们把菜送上山吧。

章七爷　等等!

众　人　么事啊?

章七爷　有个事情我要找你们调查调查。

彩　霞　七爷,你还有么事要调查?

章七爷　他们泥巴都要调查,我人为么事不能调查啊?

众　人　调查哪个?你讲啊!

[Zhang Qiye shouts inside: "Girls!"

Girls　　Qiye is coming!

Ershunzi　　Qiye is coming! (on hearing that Qiye is coming, Ershunzi runs off the stage)

Caixia　　Qiye, why are you carrying so much food up the mountain today?

Zhang Qiye　　Two bosses come to our village and say they will invest in the mountains. So, Director Xie is receiving them and asks me to bring some food here. After a while, they will come up the mountain to have a look, and Director Xie will invite them to stay for dinner on the mountain.

Sanchun　　The director of the farm needs money for road building, so it's good to have investment.

Zhang Qiye　　I'm not going up. You bring them up for me.

Girls　　OK, come on! Let's send the food up the mountain.

Zhang Qiye　　Wait a moment!

Girls　　What's the matter?

Zhang Qiye　　There is surveying I want to do to you.

Caixia　　Qiye, what do you want to survey?

Zhang Qiye　　They even survey the mud, why can't I survey a person?

Girls　　Which person will you survey? Who?

章七爷　啊，从前哪，毛主席曾经讲过，没有调查就不能瞎讲，啊，因此呢，我要调查……你们说对不对啊？

禾　香　哎呀，七爷，你倒是快讲呀！

章七爷　听说你们林场来了个姓周的什么年轻专家，是不是啊？有人告诉我，他上山就是来骗我家兰兰的。你们都说说看，有没有这事啊？

［众人像炸了窝，七嘴八舌："肯定又是章五姑在嚼舌头了""胡说八道""像这样的年轻人你想找都找不着""他一心一意帮助兰兰""人好又帅气"……

章七爷　哎哟，好着，把我的头都吵昏着，我一个一个问，你们一个一个地讲！

众姑娘　好……

章七爷　（唱）我要问他说话做事可有分寸？

彩　霞　（唱）彬彬有礼是个好书生。

章七爷　（唱）我还问种植专业可有水准？

爱　莲　（唱）兰兰有了好顾问。

Zhang Qiye — Chairman Mao once said, "without survey, one can't talk". Ah, so, um, I'll survey... Do you think it's right?

Hexiang — Yeah, Qiye, what is it?

Zhang Qiye — I hear that a young expert surnamed Zhou has come to the tree farm, right? A little bird tells me that he's here to cheat my Lanlan. Is it true?

[The girls seem to be in disarray, all talking at once. "It must be Zhang Wugu tittle-tattling again" "Nonsense" "You can't find a young man like this anymore" "He helps Lanlan wholeheartedly" "He is nice and handsome"...

Zhang Qiye — Whoops, okay, you're making me addleheaded. Let me ask you one by one, and you tell me one by one.

Girls — Okay...

Zhang Qiye — (sing) I want to ask if he behaves with propriety?

Caixia — (sing) He's a refined and courteous scholar.

Zhang Qiye — (sing) I also want to ask if he's professional?

Ailian — (sing) Lanlan has a good adviser.

章七爷　(唱)我还问吃苦耐劳他可行?

禾　香　(唱)他为人节俭又勤奋。

章七爷　(唱)还要问他可有抱负和理想?

三　春　(唱)他愿为林业献青春,

众　人　(唱)他愿为林业献青春。

章七爷　(唱)从此七爷我放了心,

众　人　(唱)你一觉睡到大天明。

章七爷　哈哈哈,听你们这么一讲啊,我就放心着。有机会,我一定要找那个章五姑评理去。

众姑娘　对,评理去!

章七爷　姑娘们啊,我走了啊!

众　人　七爷慢走!七爷走好!(收光)

[林场办公室。

[章兰兰把一块旧布铺在桌子上,哑婶来,告诉章兰兰,大意“我现在就去准备饭菜”,章兰兰做手势,大意“烧壶开水,一会客人要喝茶”。哑婶下。

Zhang Qiye	(sing) I also ask if he is a hardy person?
Hexiang	(sing) He is frugal and hardworking.
Zhang Qiye	(sing) And I also ask if he's ambitious and ideal?
Sanchun	(sing) He offers his youth to forestry,
Girls	(sing) He offers his youth to forestry.
Zhang Qiye	(sing) From now on, I'm relieved about him.
Girls	(sing) You can have a deep sleep till dawn.
Zhang Qiye	Hahaha! I can rest assured when I hear you say so! If I have a chance, I must have it out with Zhang Wugu!
Girls	Yes, have it out with her!
Zhang Qiye	Girls, I have to leave now!
Girls	Qiye, mind your step! Qiye, mind how you go! (Light gathers)

[At the office of the tree farm.

[Zhang Lanlan spreads a piece of old cloth on the table. Yashen comes to show Zhang Lanlan that she is going to cook. Zhang Lanlan makes gestures to ask her to boil a pot of water for the guests to make tea later. Yashen goes offstage.

章兰兰　(向屋内)立凡,立凡!

周立凡　(手里捧着一颗小苗)兰兰你看,这颗红豆杉的小苗已经成活了。嘿,这可是金凤林场最有价值的树种,一旦移植成功,将产生巨大的生态效益和经济效益,两个字"开心"。

章兰兰　三个字"不开心"。

周立凡　为什么?

章兰兰　你一直对我保密,把树种藏在箱底瞒着我。

周立凡　哎,可我最终还不是告诉你了。可你,我很早就想问你,一个女孩子为什么喜欢林业,你……

章兰兰　不说了,来金凤林场考察投资的人,马上就要到了,我还要准备准备呢。哎呀,叫我怎么跟他们谈呢,我真不知道说什么好。立凡,还是你出面谈吧!

周立凡　你是场长,当然由你去谈,今天只能是先摸摸底,了解一下情况,不过最主要还是看对方的实力和诚意。

章兰兰　实力和诚意?

Zhang Lanlan	(towards the inside of the house) Lifan, Lifan!
Zhou Lifan	(holding a seedling in his hands) Lanlan, look, this yew seedling has survived. Hey, this will be the most valuable tree in Jinfeng Tree Farm. Once transplanted successfully, it will produce great ecological and economic benefits. I'm so happy!
Zhang Lanlan	But, I'm not!
Zhou Lifan	Why not?
Zhang Lanlan	You have kept it a secret from me, hiding the seeds at the bottom of your suitcase.
Zhou Lifan	Hey, but I've finally told you that. But how about you? I have wanted to ask you for a long time why a girl likes forestry, you...
Zhang Lanlan	Forget it. Those who come to Jinfeng Tree Farm for investment opportunities are coming soon, and I need to get prepared for it. Oh, how am I supposed to talk with them? I don't know what to say. Lifan, how about you speak on my behalf?
Zhou Lifan	Since you are the director of the farm, of course, it's you who should talk with them. Today we can only find out and know the real situation first. The most important thing is to see the strength and sincerity of the other side.
Zhang Lanlan	Strength and sincerity?

周立凡　对！兰兰，今天光照太强，我去测试一下红豆杉土壤的水分，我马上就会回来。

章兰兰　立凡，路上小心！

周立凡　哦，那条路也在林场投资的预算里面，要想富先修路。我们要建设高标准的林场，这条路非修不可！如果村里出一部分劳力，最少也得一百万，祝兰兰谈判成功！

章兰兰　快去快回！

周立凡　是！（下）

谢主任　柳夫人，请请请！

章兰兰　谢主任！

谢主任　兰兰哪，我来介绍一下，这位是柳夫人，这位是唐秘书！

章兰兰　柳夫人，唐小姐，欢迎你们！

谢主任　这位是我们金凤林场场长章兰兰，大学毕业，很能干！

刘惠芹　哟，没想到章场长年轻漂亮，办这么大一个林场可真不容易啊！

章兰兰　柳夫人，唐秘书，请坐！

Zhou Lifan	Right! Lanlan, the light is too strong today. I'm going to test the soil moisture, and I'll be back soon.
Zhang Lanlan	Lifan, be careful on the way!
Zhou Lifan	Oh, that road is also included in the budget of farm investment. We all know that if you want to be rich, build a road first. Since we want to build a high standard tree farm, this road must be built. It will cost at least one million yuan even if the village provides labor support. Wish Lanlan a successful negotiation!
Zhang Lanlan	Come back soon!
Zhou Lifan	Yes! (go offstage)
Director Xie	Mrs. Liu, please!
Zhang Lanlan	Director Xie!
Director Xie	Lanlan, let me make an introduction. This is Mrs. Liu and this is Secretary Tang.
Zhang Lanlan	Mrs. Liu, Miss Tang, you're welcome!
Director Xie	This is Zhang Lanlan, Director of Jinfeng Tree Farm. She is a college graduate and very capable!
Liu Huiqin	Oh, I didn't expect you to be young and beautiful. It's not easy to build such a large tree farm!
Zhang Lanlan	Mrs. Liu, Miss Tang, please have a seat!

谢主任　柳夫人,来来来,坐坐坐!

章兰兰　林场刚刚起步,一切从零开始。看我这房子,你们就知道了。这还是我爷爷二十世纪六七十年代亲手造的,破旧不堪。不过我们有决心在不远的将来把这里办成一个现代化的林场!

刘惠芹　难道你哥哥就住这样的房子?

章兰兰　柳夫人,你是说……

周立娜　夫人是说,她以前也住过这样的房子!

刘惠芹　是啊是啊!

谢主任　柳夫人,你可以看看这张规划图。几年以后,这里要建休闲山庄、苗木基地、十里花溪,还有山间公园,又是天然氧吧,又是绿色银行。你们如果愿意投资的话,回报肯定没问题。兰兰哪,你和柳夫人好好谈谈,我还要去开个会,我走了啊!

章兰兰　只要投资,回报肯定没问题!

刘惠芹　我连儿子都搭进去了,我的投资还小吗?

章兰兰　柳夫人……

Director Xie	Mrs. Liu, come and sit down.
Zhang Lanlan	The tree farm has just started and everything starts from scratch. Look at my house and you'll see. It was built by my grandfather in the 1960s and 70s and was dilapidated. But we're determined to turn the tree farm into a modern one in the near future!
Liu Huiqin	So your brother lives in such a house?
Zhang Lanlan	Mrs. Liu, you're saying that...
Zhou Lina	Oh, she's saying that she has also lived in such a house before.
Liu Huiqin	It's true.
Director Xie	Mrs. Liu, you can have a look at this plan. A few years later, here will be a leisure villa, a seedling base, a ten-mile flowery stream and a hill park as well as a natural oxygen bar and a green bank. If you are willing to invest, the return is almost guaranteed. Lanlan, have a good talk with Liu. I'm going to have a meeting. I'm leaving!
Zhang Lanlan	If you invest, the return is guaranteed.
Liu Huiqin	I even put my son in it. Is my investment small?
Zhang Lanlan	Mrs. Liu...

周立娜　夫人是说，早点把资金打进去，投资不能太小啊！

刘惠芹　你哥哥人呢？

周立娜　妈，你不要着急，我有办法叫他出来。章场长，我们夫人说这里很有发展前途，不过……

章兰兰　有什么想法请讲！

周立娜　场长，

（唱）我陪夫人来考察，

果然是人杰地灵的好地方。

兰兰场长有魄力，

堪称高学历的实干家。

只是这山高沟长地盘大，

势单力薄恐难开发。

章兰兰　唐小姐，

（唱）一人难唱一台戏，

龙舟竞渡众人划。

刚刚创业难度大，

Zhou Lina	She's saying that the funds should be made earlier and the investment can't be too small!
Liu Huiqin	Where is your brother?
Zhou Lina	Don't worry, mom. I have a way to get him out. Director Zhang, Mrs. Liu says this place has a promising prospect, but...
Zhang Lanlan	Please tell me what you think!
Zhou Lina	Director,
	(sing) Madam and I inspect this place. It's really a fair place with outstanding people. You are enterprising and Can be called a highly educated doer. However, the large area of mountains and ditches Makes it hard to be developed alone!
Zhang Lanlan	Miss Tang,
	(sing) It's hard to act a play alone, Just like dragon boat races need hands. It's hard to start a business,

栽下的梧桐树先为凤凰安个家。

挥动银锄汗水洒，

荒山植树又种茶。

辛勤劳动换来丛山绿，

来年邀你赏百花。

周立娜　场长，

（唱）信息时代非以往，

单凭苦干效率差。

现代林业靠科技，

缺少人才岂不是空话。

章兰兰　干事业，当然要人才，你们可能怀疑我的软实力！你们看，这张规划图就是我们自己设计的！

刘惠芹　是你自己设计的？

章兰兰　我也会，但做不到这样精准！

周立娜　花钱请人设计的吧？

章兰兰　你们放心，我们林场有这样的人才！

Just like one should plant plane trees first to attract phoenixes.

Now we sweat hard to plant trees

And teas on barren mountains.

The next year hard work brings lush mountains,

I'll invite you to enjoy flowers.

Zhou Lina Director,

(sing) In the information age,

Hard work alone isn't efficient.

Modern forestry can't leave

Science and technology and talents!

Zhang Lanlan Of course, we need talents for our career. You may doubt my soft power. You see, this plan is designed by ourselves!

Liu Huiqin Is it designed by you?

Zhang Lanlan I can, too. But I can't be so precise!

Liu Huiqin Maybe you paid someone to design it?

Zhang Lanlan You can rest assured that there are such talents at our tree farm!

周立娜　场长，说出来别见怪，你们林场这样苦，真有人才，能留得住吗？

章兰兰　别急，等一会儿，我让你们见见我们的周设计师！

刘惠芹　立凡？（立凡内应“哎！”正好回屋）

周立凡　哎！兰兰，我回来啦！

刘惠芹　儿子！

周立凡　妈，立娜，怎么是你们？我在这里……

刘惠芹　儿子，什么都别说了，跟妈回去！

周立凡　妈……

周立娜　哥哥，你离家出走后，妈妈都急疯了，爸爸也整天吃不下饭，睡不着觉，人都瘦了不少。

章兰兰　立凡，这是怎么回事？你快说啊！

周立凡　兰兰，对不起！我没有把离家出走的事告诉你！

章兰兰　你为什么要瞒着我，你为什么不对我说实话？

刘惠芹　你们不要在我面前演戏啦！章兰兰，你装什么糊涂？就是你这个小妖精，在网上花言巧语勾引我儿子！

Zhou Lina	Director, please forgive me if I say so. Since life is so hard in your tree farm, do any talents really stay here?
Zhang Lanlan	Take it easy, and wait a moment. I'll let you meet our designer, Zhou!
Liu Huiqin	Lifan? (Lifan answers inside "Hey!" He happens to come back to the room)
Zhou Lifan	Hey, Lanlan. I'm coming back!
Liu Huiqin	My son!
Zhou Lifan	Mom, Lina! Why are you here? I'm here...
Liu Huiqin	Son! Don't say anything and go home with me!
Zhou Lifan	Mom...
Zhou Lina	Brother, since you ran away from home, mom has almost gone crazy! And dad also couldn't feel like eating and sleeping all day. He's lost a lot of weight.
Zhang Lanlan	Lifan, what's going on here? Tell me quickly!
Zhou Lifan	Lanlan, I'm sorry! I didn't tell you that I ran away from home!
Zhang Lanlan	Why did you hide it from me? Why haven't you told me the truth?
Liu Huiqin	You, stop acting in front of me! Zhang Lanlan, why are you pretending to be confused? It's you the little goblin who has seduced my son with your wiles online!

周立凡　妈，你不要污蔑章兰兰！到这里完全是我自己的决定。

刘惠芹　儿子啊，我们把你养大容易吗？自你走后，妈就像得了一场大病，每晚做梦都会梦到你，常常半夜里都会哭醒。你爸也是寝食难安，整天守在电话机前发呆。儿子啊，你就可怜可怜我们吧！

周立娜　哥哥……

章兰兰　立凡，回去吧。做人哪，什么都能忘记，唯独不能忘记父母的养育之恩啊！

周立娜　场长说的对！

周立凡　妈，我在林场想干一番事业，体现自己的人生价值，靠自己的能力体面地生活，不也是对父母的一种回报吗？更何况，金凤林场对我寄予厚望，我是一个立下过誓言的人啊！

刘惠芹　立凡，妈已经把话说尽了。我向你挑明了说，给你三天时间，三天后你若再不回家，那你就在这山上准备一块墓地。妈就是死，也要看着你！

Zhou Lifan	Mom, don't get her wrong! It is entirely my own decision to come here.
Liu Huiqin	My son, is it easy for us to bring you up? Since you left home, I've been like suffering from a serious illness. I dream of you every night and often wake up in the middle of night crying. Your dad also stays up at night with worry, and is in a daze in front of the phone all day. Lifan, take pity on us!
Zhou Lina	Brother...
Zhang Lanlan	Lifan, go back. We can forget anything, but not our parents' love and care we received from childhood.
Zhou Lina	She's right!
Zhou Lifan	Mom, I want to make a career in the tree farm, realize my life value, and live a decent life by my own ability. Isn't it also a kind of return to my parents? Moreover, Jinfeng Tree Farm places great expectations on me. I'm a man who has made a promise!
Liu Huiqin	Lifan, I've said all I have to say. I make it clear to you that I'll just give you three days to consider it. If you will not go home after three days, you will need to prepare a cemetery on this mountain. Mom would watch you even if I died!

周立娜　妈……（二幕下）

［兰兰和立凡的心被刺痛，两人同时来到舞台前沿。二幕下，掩去了其余所有人。

周立凡　兰兰，我不该瞒着你，我对不起你，让你受到伤害！

章兰兰　回去吧，我也不想责怪你，只要你生活得好，我会高兴的……美好的回忆兴许会使我的心情更敞亮一些！

（唱）我满腔热情办林场，

周立凡　（唱）绿色的精灵在歌唱。

章兰兰　（唱）你匆匆来到我身边，

周立凡　（唱）创业的激情在飞扬。

章兰兰　（唱）面对青山发誓愿，

周立凡　（唱）青春无悔追希望。

章兰兰　（唱）一撇一捺绘蓝图，

周立凡　（唱）一锹一锄写篇章。

章兰兰　（唱）汗水洒下地生金，

周立凡　（唱）只为来年百花香。

Zhou Lina	Mom... (the second curtain falls)

[Feeling their hearts stung, Lanlan and Lifan both come to the front of the stage at the same time. The second curtain falls to cover the others.

Zhou Lifan	Lanlan, I shouldn't have kept it from you. I'm sorry for hurting you!
Zhang Lanlan	Go back. I don't want to blame you. If live well, I'll be glad... Good memories may make me feel brighter!
	(sing) I build the tree farm with great zest,
Zhou Lifan	(sing) Where green elves are singing happily.
Zhang Lanlan	(sing) You came to my side in a hurry
Zhou Lifan	(sing) With passion to start a business.
Zhang Lanlan	(sing) I made a vow to mountains,
Zhou Lifan	(sing) I'd chase hope without regrets.
Zhang Lanlan	(sing) Draw the blueprint earnestly,
Zhou Lifan	(sing) Realize the dream arduously.
Zhang Lanlan	(sing) We water the ground with our sweat
Zhou Lifan	(sing) Just for fragrant flowers next year.

章兰兰　(唱)谁知一场风波起,

周立凡　(唱)何去何从两彷徨。

[在一阵鸟鸣和虚幻的音乐声中,二幕徐徐升起。兰兰和立凡来到了秀美的山谷边,面对风和日丽的景色,二人进入了回忆。

章兰兰　立凡,你真的愿意和我在一起办林场吗?

周立凡　兰兰,你还在怀疑我吗?

章兰兰　你有才华,应该到城市,到科研院所去发展,窝在山沟里,岂不是太可惜了!

周立凡　兰兰,你也很优秀,不当白领,回乡办林场不可惜吗?我要用我学到的知识来改变这里的面貌,我们俩携手建成一座高标准的大林场,也算不虚度年华了!

章兰兰　心里话?

周立凡　心里话!

章兰兰　不后悔?

周立凡　不后悔!

章兰兰　拉钩?

Zhang Lanlan (sing) But who knows a trouble appears

Zhou Lifan (sing) And I wonder where to go.

[Amidst the singing of birds and the sound of illusory music, the second curtain rises slowly. Lanlan and Lifan come to a beautiful valley and enter memories in which there are a fine view with gentle breezes and bright sunshine.

Zhang Lanlan Lifan, do you really want to build the tree farm with me?

Zhou Lifan Lanlan, are you still doubting me?

Zhang Lanlan You are talented. You should go to the big city or a research institute to develop yourself. Isn't it a great pity for you to stay in this gully?

Zhou Lifan Lanlan, you are also very outstanding. Isn't it a pity for you not to become a white-collar but to come back to the countryside to build the tree farm? I will use the knowledge I've learned to change the face of this place. If we work together to build a high-standard tree farm, our time will pay off!

Zhang Lanlan To be honest?

Zhou Lifan Yes!

Zhang Lanlan Not regret?

Zhou Lifan No!

Zhang Lanlan Pinky-swear?

周立凡　拉钩！

［二人拉钩，兰兰趔趄，被立凡扶住，兰兰害羞地推开立凡。

章兰兰　立凡，

（唱）自你来到我身边，
一颗心儿不再悬。
多了一根主心骨，
信心倍增劲更添。
先前常觉担子重，
食不甘来夜难安。
从今后一副担子两人挑，
兰兰可以歇歇肩。

周立凡　（唱）魂牵梦绕是青山，
来到青山慰我愿。
远离喧嚣多惬意，
坐看云舒百鸟喧。
兰兰啊，你匠心独具有慧眼，
识得深闺好洞天。

Zhou Lifan　　Pinky-swear!

[The two make pinky-swear. Lanlan staggered and was held up by Lifan, and Lanlan shyly pushed Lifan away.

Zhang Lanlan　Lifan,

(sing) Ever since you came to my side,
I've no longer felt worried.
You are my new backbone which
Doubles my confidence and strength.
I often felt the burden heavy,
So, I couldn't eat and sleep well.
From now on two people can share the burden,
Lanlan can rest the shoulders.

Zhou Lifan　　(sing) Lush mountains appeal to me
So that I meet my wishes here.
Pleased to be away from bustle,
I sit and watch clouds and birds.
Oh Lanlan, you're original and insightful
To choose the unknown good place.

我与你荒山野岭播绿色，
双手营造新家园。
兰兰啊，人生可贵是作为，
青春做伴苦亦甜。
开弓没有回头箭，
天道酬勤石也穿。
兰兰啊，一颗心儿交给你，
心心相印到百年。

章兰兰　（唱）到百年！

[二幕下，形成幕里幕外的格局，兰兰在里，立凡在外。

章兰兰　立凡，回去吧！回去后，多陪你爸妈说说话，让他们能宽宽心！

周立凡　兰兰，我走后，最放心不下的就是那片红豆杉，小苗刚出土，枝叶还小，你一定要好好照看！

（唱）南国生长的红豆杉，
北移林场成夙愿。

You and me, sow green in barren mountains,
And create a new home with hands.
Oh Lanlan, the valuable in life is doing,
Youth company makes bitter sweet.
As what's done can't be undone,
God helps those who help themselves.
Oh Lanlan, I devote my heart to you,
Wishing we're both of the same mind.

Zhang Lanlan (sing) The same mind.

[The second curtain falls to form a pattern in which Lanlan is inside while Lifan is outside.

Zhang Lanlan Lifan, go back! Go back to talk with your parents and set their mind at ease!

Zhou Lifan Lanlan, after I leave, what worries me most are those yews. The seedlings just sprout and the branches and leaves are still tender. You must take good care of them!

(sing) I've long wished to move the yews
From the south to the north farm.

留给兰兰做纪念，
愿它扎根在青山。

章兰兰　（唱）提起红豆泪潸潸，
今生不枉识立凡。
倘若日后难聚首，
不忘你赠我红豆杉。

[二幕下。

（伴唱）冷月清辉万籁寂，
相思红豆意绵绵。

[收光。

Leave it here as a keepsake,

May it take root in mountains.

Zhang Lanlan (sing) Hearing of Taxus I cry,

For I know you in my life.

If we couldn't meet in future,

I wouldn't forget your Taxus.

[The second curtain falls.

(chorus) In the moonlight and silence,

Their lovesickness is endless.

[Light gathers.

第五场

[二顺子身背工具包，从下场门上。章七爷从上场门上，章七爷手拿写字夹板和笔，数数记记，显然他在清点山上的树。二顺子见章七爷，转身就跑，被章七爷看见。

章七爷　（哼唱）桐城呐，六尺巷，美名传四方，有人问你有多长，气度怎可量？

二顺子　（哼唱）你是我的小呀小苹果……

章七爷　山上有老虎哦！

二顺子　真有老虎啊？

章七爷　我就是老虎嘛！要不然，你见了我就跑么事呢？

二顺子　我……

章七爷　二顺子啊，你呀，是碰到一个好村主任，硬是让你学好了！

二顺子　七爷，你不也学好了吗？还当了个大官！

章七爷　不错，金凤林场护林组总顾问！

Act Ⅴ

[Ershunzi goes on the stage from the Stage Left, carrying the tool bag on his back, while Zhang Qiye goes on the stage from the Stage Right, holding a writing board and a pen in his hand, counting and writing. Obviously, he was counting the trees on the mountain. On seeing Zhang Qiye, Ershunzi turns around to run away and is seen by Zhang Qiye.

Zhang Qiye (humming) Tongcheng is famous for the Lane of Courtesy.
When asked about its length, how to measure tolerance?

Ershunzi (humming) You are my little, little apple...

Zhang Qiye There are tigers on the mountain!

Ershunzi Are there tigers really?

Zhang Qiye I am the tiger. Otherwise, why do you run away when you see me?

Ershunzi Well...

Zhang Qiye Ershunzi, you met a good village committee director, who really manages to make you follow good examples!

Ershunzi Qiye, don't you follow good examples, too? Now you even become a high official!

Zhang Qiye Yes, I am the General Adviser of the Forest Protection Team of Jinfeng Tree Farm!

二顺子　嘿嘿嘿，七爷，没有那个总字，就是顾问！

章七爷　我叫加的嘛，兰兰都同意了，关你么事啊！

二顺子　好好好，报告总顾问，兰兰场长说林场配电板出了故障，叫我去修理，我去了啊！

章七爷　去吧，去吧！

二顺子　我去了啊！

［二顺子刚要走，巧珍在彩霞与三春的陪同下上场。巧珍身上背一个包，三春替她拎着一只箱子，巧珍抹着泪。

章七爷　巧珍呀，你回来啦？

巧　珍　七爷……（哭）

章七爷　回来就好，回来就好！那个章五姑呢？

巧　珍　派出所的人说，她还要接受进一步调查，说我已经没有问题。你们不会看不起我吧？

二顺子　不会，不会哟！

章七爷　丫头啊，你们场长正记挂着你呢！她说只要你回来，我们会对你更好的！

Ershunzi Hey, hey, hey, Qiye, you are just an adviser, not the general adviser!

Zhang Qiye I asked Lanlan for this title and she agreed. It's none of your business!

Ershunzi Well, well, dear General Adviser, Director Lanlan says that something is wrong with the switchboard of the tree farm and she asks me to repair it. I'm going to do it now!

Zhang Qiye Go ahead, go ahead!

Ershunzi I'm going now!

[When Ershunzi is about to leave, Qiaozhen goes onstage, accompanied by Caixia and Sanchun. Qiaozhen is wiping her tears, with a bag on her back while Sanchun is carrying a suitcase for her.

Zhang Qiye Qiaozhen, you are back?

Qiaozhen Qiye... (crying)

Zhang Qiye It's good as long as you're back. What about Zhang Wugu?

Qiaozhen The police officers say that she still needs further investigation and that nothing is wrong with me. Will you look down on me?

Ershunzi No, we won't!

Zhang Qiye Oh, girl, the director of the farm worries about you! She says as long as you come back, we will treat you better!

二顺子　(赶紧取过包,拿过箱子)对对对,场长是说过这话,我们会对你更好的,我来。

章七爷　哎！别人都能讲这句话,你二顺子不能讲!

彩　霞　七爷,你管那么多闲事做么事啊。走,上山去哟!

二顺子　回来就好,走走走!(下场,收光)

周立凡　(唱)伫立窗前望青山,
不见青山见夕阳。
耳畔似有人声唤,
兰兰啊!
我分明是难舍难忘。
你的倩影挥不去,
一日不见如三秋长。
回家却有陌生感,
我与父母隔堵墙。
父亲他重话不敢讲,
母亲她青丝添白霜。

Ershunzi (take the bag and the suitcase from the girls in a hurry) Yes, yes, yes, it's the words of the director of the farm. We will treat you better! Let me do it.

Zhang Qiye Hey! Others can say these words. But you can't!

Caixia Qiye, why do you get your nose in everything? Come on, go up to the mountain!

Ershunzi It's good as long as you're back! Let's go! Let's go! (go offstage. light gathers)

Zhou Lifan (sing) I stand by the window to
See no mountains but sunset.
I seem to hear someone call.
Oh, Lanlan,
It's clear that I can't forget you.
Your pretty shadow does not go away,
It's absence that sharpens my love.
I'm back with a strange feeling
Of being walled off from parents.
Father does not dare to have harsh words
And mother finds her black hair turn grey.

扪心自问我实实欠妥当，
他们的护犊深情要体谅。
幸有小妹周立娜，
苦心相劝摆短长。
亲情能解千千结[38]，
柳暗花明有希望。
拿出手机把话讲，
电波传情到她身旁。

[二幕下。

周立凡　喂，喂，兰兰是我呀！

章兰兰　喂，是天马吗？

周立凡　你怎么又叫我天马了？

章兰兰　我想，我们还是回到见面前的状态更好些！

周立凡　为什么？

章兰兰　这还用问吗？你懂的。

周立凡　我真的不懂，兰兰，不过我想告诉你，现在情况有些转机，主要原因是我妹妹周立娜就要成为你的粉丝啦！

By Asking myself, I was entirely wrong.
I should have understood their parental love.
Thanks to my sister Lina
Who tried hard to persuade them.
Family love can solve problems[38],
Things will turn for the better.
Take out my phone to call her,
Sending her my love through radio waves.

[The second curtain falls.

Zhou Linfan	Hello, hello, Lanlan, it's me!
Zhang Lanlan	Hello, is that Tianma?
Zhou Linfan	Why do you call me Tianma again?
Zhang Lanlan	I think it would be better for us to remain the state before we met!
Zhou Linfan	Why?
Zhang Lanlan	You know why and you know what I mean.
Zhou Linfan	No, I don't. But I want to tell you, Lanlan, that there is a change for the better mainly because my sister Zhou Lina is about to become your fan!

章兰兰　你胡说，我又不是明星！

周立凡　兰兰！

（唱）人非草木孰无情，

你善良勤奋已经拨动她年轻的心。

章兰兰　（唱）纵然立娜心底明，

你的父母未必是知音。

周立凡　（唱）古人云，天时人事日相催[39]，

枯木也能枝芽新。

兰兰不信我的话，

偷拍的视频为佐证。

（白）兰兰，请你打开视频。

［舞台纱幕后的一个表演区出现周立娜、周志豪、刘惠芹。

周立娜　爸妈，如果你们连自己的亲生女儿都不相信，那你们只有把章五姑从看守所请到家里好好商量一下，下一步该怎么办？

周志豪　你也亲眼看到了。章五姑说她像狐狸精，她到底像不像？

Zhang Lanlan You are talking nonsense. I'm not a star!

Zhou Linfan Lanlan!

(sing) How can we be ruthless plants?

It is your kindness and diligence that have touched her young heart.

Zhang Lanlan (sing) Even though Lina understands me,

Your parents may not be my bosom friends.

Zhou Linfan (sing) The ancients said that time flies so quickly[39],

And dead woods can shoot new branches.

If you don't believe my words,

The candid video can be my proof.

(speak) Lanlan, pleaseconnect the video call.

[Zhou Lina, Zhou Zhihao and Liu Huiqin appear in a performance area behind the lace curtain of the stage.

Zhou Lina Dad, mom, if you don't believe your own daughter, you have to go to the police station to invite Zhang Wugu home and have a good discussion with her about what we should do next.

Zhou Zhihao You've also seen her with your own eyes. Zhang Wugu said she looks like a foxtrel. Does she look like a foxtrel or not?

刘惠芹　不太像！

周立娜　人家长得漂亮就说人家是狐狸精，这公平吗？再说章兰兰知情知理，她说做人什么都能忘，就是不能忘记父母的养育之恩，是她劝哥哥回家的。她年纪轻轻，管理着那么大一片山林，这要付出多少艰辛啊！

周志豪　你为什么不早说呢？

周立娜　妈妈整天守着你，她也没说呀！

周志豪　对，还有你！为什么不早说呀？

刘惠芹　我是怕立凡又回到林场去，山上实在太苦了！

周志豪　我养王八不苦吗？哪个不是从吃苦中过来的，要是当初你嫌弃我，我们早就拆开了。

刘惠芹　现在还来得及，拆开、拆开……

周志豪　你……

［画面定格，渐渐收去，他俩继续通话。

周立凡　兰兰，刚才的视频精彩吗？

章兰兰　还算精彩！不过，你怎么干起了狗仔队的勾当？

Liu Huiqin Not so much!

Zhou Lina Is it fair to call someone a foxtrel if someone is beautiful? Besides, Zhang Lanlan is reasonable and sensible. She said that no one should forget the loving kindness of their parents. And it was she who persuaded my brother to come back home. How hard it must have been for her to manage so large a forestry farm at such a young age!

Zhou Zhihao Why didn't you tell me earlier?

Zhou Lina Mom has been with you the whole day and she didn't tell you either!

Zhou Zhihao Yes, and you, why didn't you tell me earlier?

Liu Huiqin I was afraid that Lifan would go back to the tree farm again. The living conditions on the mountains are too hard!

Zhou Zhihao Isn't it hard for me to farm soft-shelled turtles? Everyone needs to work hard. If you had despised me at the beginning, we would have broken up early.

Liu Huiqin It's still not too late. Break up, break up...

Zhou Zhihao You...

[The picture freezes and fades away, and they continue to talk.

Zhou Lifan Lanlan, was the video wonderful?

Zhang Lanlan Yes, it was! But why did you work as paparazzi?

周立凡　真情可以融化坚冰,请相信你的魅力,也相信我的能力!

章兰兰　立凡,我只相信梦中那一片郁郁葱葱的山林!

周立凡　和我一样！哎,兰兰,快到雷雨季节了,那片红豆杉的幼苗,可要做好防范措施,一定要保护好!

章兰兰　放心,我还有事,你先挂!

周立凡　你先挂!

章兰兰　我们一起挂,一、二、三!

[在"一、二、三"中收光。

ZhouLifan	True love can melt ice. Please believe in my ability as well as your charm!
Zhang Lanlan	Lifan, I only believe in the lush and luxuriant wooded mountains in my dream!
Zhou Lifan	Me too! Lanlan, the thunderstorm season is coming, so you must take precautions against the storm and protect those yew seedlings well!
Zhang Lanlan	Don't worry. I have something else to do. You hang up first!
Zhou Lifan	You hang up first!
Zhang Lanlan	Let's hang up together. One, two, three!

[Light gathers in the sound of "one, two, three".

第六场

[雷声轰鸣,暴雨倾盆。

[二幕前,有人扛着木桩,有人背着背篓,有人撑着雨伞,匆匆过往。

谢主任　二顺子,那边的电线杆已经倒伏,你快去拉掉电闸,保证上山抢险人员的安全!

二顺子　是!

谢主任　走!(下)

[村民过场。

谢主任　村民们,风大雨急,千万要当心山上的滚石,大家要小心哪!(下)

[二幕起,红豆杉的种植地。

[章兰兰冒雨前行,一会儿跌倒,一会儿攀登。当她奋力地爬到红豆杉苗圃的小山坡时,她惊呆了,原来立凡早就在小苗周围打下了木桩,扶正了小苗。

Act Ⅵ

[Thunder roars and rain pours down.

[In front of the second curtain, people are passing by in a hurry, with some carrying wooden stakes on their shoulders, some carrying baskets on their backs, and some holding umbrellas.

Director Xie　　Ershunzi, the wire pole over there has fallen. Be quick to turn off the switch! Ensure the safety of rescuers going up the mountain!

Ershunzi　　Yes, sir!

Director Xie　　Go! (go offstage)

[Villagers walk through the scene.

Director Xie　　Villagers, the wind is strong and the rain is heavy. Watch out for rolling stones on the mountain! Everyone must be careful! (go offstage)

[The second curtain goes up. At the Taxus seedling base.

[Zhang Lanlan presses forward in the rain, keep falling but continuing to climb uphill. While she struggles to climb to the hillside yew seedling base, she was shocked. It turns out that Lifan has already laid down wooden stakes around the seedlings and straightens the seedlings.

周立凡　兰兰，我先到一步，来不及告诉你，我已经把它们全部绑好了！

章兰兰　（惊呆良久，她突然发疯般地扑过去，紧紧地抱住立凡）立凡，你什么时候来的？怎么不告诉我一声？

周立凡　听到天气预报说今天这里有暴雨，我是提前来的，所以我们的红豆杉安然无恙，你放心吧！

章兰兰　只要有你在，我还有什么不放心的。不过，这次你不会又是离家出走吧？

周立凡　爸爸和妹妹支持我，妈妈不同意，二比一，我被通过了！

章兰兰　你妈妈的心情你也该理解啊！

周立凡　那就要看你的魅力啦！

章兰兰　去，一个山村女娃子，你说有什么魅力？

周立凡　魅力无穷，光芒四射，哈哈哈！

章兰兰　滚石！

[突然一阵石块滚落声，兰兰奋力将立凡推开，自己的手臂却被山石砸伤。

Zhou Lifan　Lanlan, I got here earlier than you. There is no time for me to tell you that I've tied them all up!

Zhang Lanlan　(after being stunned for a good while, she suddenly runs into Lifan's arms and hugs him tightly) Lifan, when did you come here? Why didn't you tell me?

Zhou Lifan　I heard the weather forecast for a torrential rain here today, so I came early. You see our yew seedlings are safe and sound. You can rest assured!

Zhang Lanlan　As long as you are here, I have nothing to worry about. But this time you're not running away from home again, are you?

Zhou Lifan　No. My father and sister support me while my mother disagrees. Two to one, I passed.

Zhang Lanlan　You have to understand your mother!

Zhou Lifan　Then it'll depend on your charm!

Zhang Lanlan　Tsk, I'm just a girl from a mountain village, what charm do you think I have?

Zhou Lifan　Charming and radiant! Ha-ha-ha!

Zhang Lanlan　Rolling stones!

[Here comes a sudden sound of rolling stones. Lanlan struggles to push Lifan away, but she is injured in the arm by a falling stone.

周立凡　兰兰……你没事吧？

章兰兰　我没事！

周立凡　血！兰兰，你流血了！

章兰兰　只是擦破了点皮，没关系！

周立凡　（为兰兰擦拭着）风雨过去了，我们歇歇再走吧，这里安全些。

章兰兰　刚才好险啊！

周立凡　是啊！要不是你救了我，我就被山上的滚石砸死了！

章兰兰　（痛哭着）滚石……砸死……

周立凡　不对，一定是你伤得很重，我背你下山！

章兰兰　不，立凡，我对你还有个秘密，记得吗？

周立凡　记得，一个女孩子为什么会喜欢林业？

章兰兰　十多年了，我想都不敢想，提都不敢提，因为……因为我只要一想起这件事，就像在我的伤口上撒了一把盐呀！

周立凡　别说了，就把它埋在心底吧！

章兰兰　可是今天我想原原本本地对你说！

Zhou Lifan	Lanlan... Are you ok?
Zhang Lanlan	I'm all right!
Zhou Lifan	Blood! Lanlan, you're bleeding!
Zhang Lanlan	Just a scratch, it's all right!
Zhou Lifan	(wipe it for Lanlan) The storm has passed. Let's rest before we go. It's safer here.
Zhang Lanlan	That was close!
Zhou Lifan	Yeah! If you hadn't saved me, I would have been smashed to death by rolling stones from the mountain!
Zhang Lanlan	(crying bitterly) Rolling stones...smashed to death...
Zhou Lifan	No, you must have been hurt badly! I'll carry you down the mountain!
Zhang Lanlan	No, Lifan, do you remember I still have a secret from you?
Zhou Lifan	Yes, why does a girl like forestry?
Zhang Lanlan	For more than ten years, I have not dared to think about it or even mention it, because... because the moment I think about it, it's just like rubbing salt into my wound!
Zhou Lifan	Then keep it a secret. Just bury it at the bottom of your heart!
Zhang Lanlan	But today I want to tell you as exact as it is!

（唱）风雨后，天边映出一抹彩霞，
逃劫难，兰兰我终把心放下。
当年的场景又重现，
向立凡诉一诉说一说，
说出那十年前的伤心话。
父母生我姐弟俩，
三岁弟弟学语丫丫。
他的小手牵着我衣裳，
要去山上采野花。
采来野花送姐姐，
采来野花送爸妈。
弟弟天真又可爱，
我们一路欢笑离了家。
那一天阳光灿烂朵朵白云天边挂，
山坡上的鸟儿叫喳喳。

(sing) After the storm, there's a rosy glow on the horizon.
The survival makes me feel relieved finally.
The reappeared scene of that year
Makes me pour out my words to Lifan.
It was a sad story happened ten years ago.
My parents had two children,
Three years old younger brother and me.
One day, he held my clothes and wanted to
Pick wild flowers on the mountain
And send them to his sister
As well as his dear parents.
He really was cute and naive.
We left home both laughing all the way
With the bright sunshine and the white clouds hanging
on the sky
And the birds chirping on the hillside.

突然间老天变了脸，
风雨如注纷纷下。
我拉着弟弟往回跑，
步步惊心山路滑。
突然间，碎石滚落遇险情，
可怜的弟弟呀，偏偏被那石块砸。
我抱着弟弟放声哭啊。
他他他紧闭双眼，
小手攥着三枝山野花。
放不下，忘不了，
一个想法出萌芽。
为什么山体裸露植被少，
是人祸竭泽而渔乱砍伐。
长大我定要学林业，
让苍茫大地披绿纱。

But suddenly the weather changed.
In the heavy downpour of rain,
I pulled my brother and ran back home.
On the slippery mountain road,
We were in danger of sudden falling stones.
My poor younger brother was just hit by a rolling stone,
I held my brother in my arms and cried.
He, he closed his eyes tightly
With three wild flowers in his little hand.
I could not forget it
So that I have sprouted an idea.
Why were the mountains barren with few plants?
It's due to human casual felling of the trees.
When grown up, I'll learn forestry
To cover the vast land with green trees.

立凡啊，你问我女孩为何要学林，
为锁住洪涝，为一片绿荫，为溪水长流，
为留住乡愁。
为生态，为环境，为绿色，为生存，
为让我弟弟看一看，
绿水青山垂杨紫陌一个美丽的家。

周立凡　兰兰，我会一辈子守着这个林场！一辈子守着这片山林！（回声）

章兰兰　立凡！

周立凡　兰兰！

章兰兰　立凡！

[二人相拥。走到台前，再回身到台后，渐收光。

Lifan, you asked me why a girl should learn forestry.

For locking the flooding, for having the shade, for the flowing streams,

For the homesickness,

For ecology, environment, the green and survival,

For letting my brother have a look

At such a beautiful home with lucid water and lush mountains.

Zhou Lifan Lanlan, I will be with this tree farm forever! I will be with this wooded mountain forever! (echo)

Zhang Lanlan Lifan!

Zhou Lifan Lanlan!

Zhang Lanlan Lifan!

[They embrace each other and walk to the front of the stage, then turn around to go to the back of the stage. The light gradually fades away.

第七场

[喜庆的音乐声中伴着鸟鸣声不绝于耳，二顺子与巧珍拉开横幅，上面写着“热烈欢迎起业家”。

巧　珍　顺子啊！

二顺子　么事？同花！[40]

巧　珍　你怎么叫我同花？

二顺子　你怎么叫我顺子！[41]

巧　珍　这样叫不亲热些吗？

二顺子　是吗？好，以后就叫我顺子，把那个二百五[42]的二[43]拿下！

巧　珍　顺子，这个企业家的“起”字，我怎么看都觉得不像！

二顺子　不像？它是不是念“起”？

巧　珍　是啊！

二顺子　是不就照迈！

巧　珍　我是怕人家会说我们没文化。

Act Ⅶ

[With the sound of festive music and the singing of birds, Ershunzi and Qiaozhen open a banner with the words "A Warm Welcome to Entrypreners".

Qiaozhen　Shunzi!

Ershunzi　What's the matter? Tonghua[40]!

Qiaozhen　Why do you call me Tonghua?

Ershunzi　Why do you call me Shunzi[41]?!

Qiaozhen　Isn't it more affectionate to call you so?

Ershunzi　Is it? Well, call me Shunzi later. Take away the "two"[42] from the "two hundred and fifty"[43]!

Qiaozhen　Shunzi, I don't think the spelling of entryprener looks like correct!

Ershunzi　Does it pronounce [ˌɒntrəprəˈnɜː]?

Qiaozhen　Yeah!

Ershunzi　Then, that's ok!

Qiaozhen　I just don't want us to appear uneducated.

二顺子　我没文化？想当年我差一点就考上了省重点中学桐中。巧珍，你说怎么改？

巧　珍　我也忘了，哎呀，来不及了，他们已经来了！

［二顺子急中生智，把“起业家”三个字折起来，变成了“热烈欢迎”。

［谢主任走在前头，刘惠芹、周立娜、周志豪随后。

谢主任　来来来，请请请，前面就到了！

周志豪　看见了吧，人家拉着横幅来欢迎我们呢，多热情啊！

谢主任　二顺子，我看你是越来越能干了。

二顺子　谢谢主任！谢主任，各位企业家一路走好！

谢主任　哦，一路走好，这话听着怎么这么别扭啊。二顺子，你跑步上山告诉场长，就说企业家已经到了，叫他们做好准备。

二顺子　是！

谢主任　请请请，山上的路不好走！

周志豪　谢主任，要是这里有一条路，我们就可以开着车上山了！

谢主任　他们早有计划，只是……还要等一等！

Ershunzi Am I uneducated? When I was younger, I was almost admitted to the provincial key middle school—Tongcheng Middle School. Qiaozhen, how do you think we should correct it?

Qiaozhen I also forget it. Oops, it's too late, they are coming!

[Ershunzi hits on an idea in desperation. He folds up the words "to entrypreners" and turns the words into "A Warm Welcome".

[Director Xie walks in the front, followed by Liu Huiqin, Zhou Lina and Zhou Zhihao.

Director Xie Come here, please, please, please. We are almost there!

Zhou Zhihao See that? People are holding a banner to welcome us. How enthusiastic they are!

Director Xie Ershunzi, I think you are getting more and more competent!

Ershunzi Thank you, Director Xie! Director Xie and entrepreneurs, wish you all the best!

Director Xie Oh, what an awkward greeting! Ershunzi, you run up the mountain to tell the director of the farm that the entrepreneurs have arrived and ask them to be ready.

Ershunzi Yes!

Director Xie Please, please, please! The mountain road is rough!

Zhou Zhihao Director Xie, if there were a road here, we can drive up to the mountain!

Director Xie They have a plan, but... we have to wait.

刘惠芹　还等么事哦！叫他爸爸给钱，以后我来看儿子还方便些！

周丽娜　还是妈妈想得周到！

周志豪　你妈妈就是卫生口罩——嘴上一套[44]。你叫她拿钱啊！

刘惠芹　你以为我拿不出啊！

周志豪　那你拿呀！

刘惠芹　拿就拿！

谢主任　唉……

周立娜　谢主任别见怪，我爸妈是吵了一辈子又好了一辈子。

谢主任　是吗？哟，他们敲锣打鼓欢迎你们呢！来来来，请请请……

周志豪　快走吧！（收光）

[二幕前，林场办公室，人很多，哑婶端茶倒水，章七爷招呼着大家。

章兰兰　大家静一静！静一静！告诉大家一个好消息，市领导已经派专人来考察过了，他们要把绿色环保、植树造林作为重要的工作来抓，我们金凤林场被列为市里的重点项目。

Liu Huiqin	Why do you have to wait? Ask his father to give you the money. It will be easier for me to visit my son in the future!
Zhou Lina	Mom is still thoughtful!
Zhou Zhihao	Your mom is just all talk without doing[44]. You ask her to give the money!
Liu Huiqin	Why don't you think I have the money?
Zhou Zhihao	Then do it.
Liu Huiqin	No problem!
Director Xie	Alas...
Zhou lina	Director Xie, no hard feelings. They just argue and then make it up all the time.
Director Xie	Really? Whee, they welcome you with drums and gongs! Come here, come here, please, please, please...
Zhou Zhihao	Hurry up! (light gathers)

[In front of the second curtain, in the office of the tree farm. There are many people in the room. Yashen is serving tea while Zhang Qiye is greeting everyone.

Zhang Lanlan	Be quiet, everybody! Be quiet! I have good news to tell everybody. The municipal leaders have sent specially-assigned persons to carry out an inspection. They will prioritize environmental protection and afforestation. Our Jinfeng Tree Farm has been listed as a key municipal project.

谢主任　还有啊，我们青山村已经被市里列为美好乡村建设省级示范村了！

众　人　好！（欢呼声）

章兰兰　今天立凡的父母作为企业家也想加入我们支持林场的发展。我们大家用热烈的掌声欢迎他们，现在请周伯父、刘阿姨说几句！

周志豪　这个……

章七爷　等等……兰兰啊，哦，不，场长还年轻，规矩啊还没有学会，我是她的爷爷，又是总顾问……

二顺子　护林小组总顾问！

章七爷　还不是总顾问嘛。她刚才叫你么东西啊？哦！老周啊，你莫见怪，我来开导开导兰兰，要叫爸爸妈妈，大家说是不是啊？

众　人　是！

章兰兰　（和谢主任交流一下）叫就叫，爸爸妈妈！

众　人　好！

章兰兰　爸妈，你们说说吧！

Director Xie	And Qingshan village has been listed as a provincial demonstration village for beautiful rural construction by the city!
Everybody	Good! (hurrah)
Zhang Lanlan	Today, Lifan's parents, as entrepreneurs, also want to join us to support the development of our tree farm. Let's welcome them with warm applause! Now let's welcome Mr. Zhou and Madame Liu to say a few words!
Zhou Zhihao	OK ...
Zhang Qiye	Wait a minute. Lanlan, ah, oh, no, the director of the farm is still young. She still hasn't learned some rules. As her grandfather, ah, as well as the General Adviser...
Ershunzi	The General Adviser of Forest Protection Group!
Zhang Qiye	I'm not General Adviser yet. What did she call you just now? Oh, Mr. Zhou, no hard feelings. Let me enlighten her. Lanlan should call them mom and dad. Don't you think so?
Everybody	Yes!
Zhang Lanlan	(talk to Director Xie) OK, dad, mom.
Everybody	Good!
Zhang Lanlan	Dad, mom, please say a few words!

周志豪　好！我不想说空话。这么大一个林场，连一条上山的路都没有，赶快修一条路，我出一百五十万！

刘惠芹　你爸爸呀，有时还真小气。我再加五十万，凑个整数，两百万，好事成双嘛！

周志豪　老婆哎，你的钱不就是我的钱吗？

刘惠芹　怎么？你心痛了？

周志豪　怎么会呢，把账号给我，明天就给你们打两百万！

彩　霞　这是我的名片，上面有林场的账号！

章七爷　我来介绍一下，她是我们金凤林场的总会计师！

二顺子　七爷，没有那个总字！

章七爷　我叫加的嘛，关你么事啊？

周立凡　谢谢爸！

周志豪　儿子啊，爸爸有时脾气不好，你也要原谅啊。过去，我一直把你当小孩子，现在才知道，你已经长大了！

周立凡　爸！

周立娜　爸！（扶周志豪坐下）

Zhou Zhihao OK! I don't want to have empty talk. For such a large tree farm, there isn't a road to go up the mountain. I'll pay 1.5 million yuan to build a road quickly!

Zhou Huiqin Your dad really is stingy sometimes! I'll give you another half a million yuan to make it a round number, two million! Good things come in pairs!

Zhou Zhihao Dear, isn't your money also mine?

Zhou Huiqin So? Does your heart hurt?

Zhou Zhihao How could? Give me your account number and I will transfer two million to you tomorrow!

Caixia This is my name card with the account number of the tree farm on it!

Zhang Qiye Let me introduce her. Caixia, the General Accountant of our Jinfeng Tree Farm!

Ershunzi Qiye, without the word General!

Zhang Qiye It's my idea to add the word. It's none of your business.

Zhou Lifan Dad, thank you.

ZhouZhihao Son, you have to forgive dad for being grumpy sometimes. I used to treat you as a child, but now I know that you've grown up!

Zhou Lifan Dad!

Zhou Lina Dad! (help Zhou Zhihao to sit down)

章兰兰　立凡！

彩　霞　哎……我代表大家提问，什么时候可以吃你们的喜糖啊？

［兰兰和立凡互看，羞涩地回头。

章七爷　他们不说啊，还是问问谢主任。谢主任啊，你说，你是我们的村主任，又是我们的书记。

谢主任　他们什么时候生小伢子我管不了，这结婚的日子嘛，我看就选在金凤林场公路竣工的那一天，我们开着车子把一对新人送入洞房，大家看怎么样啊？

众　人　好！

彩　霞　我提议让准新郎准新娘唱一段黄梅戏“夫妻双双把家还”，好不好啊？

众　人　好！

章兰兰　（唱）树上的鸟儿成双对，

周立凡　（唱）绿水青山带笑颜。

章兰兰　（唱）随手摘下花一朵，

周立凡　（唱）我与娘子戴发间。

Zhang Lanlan　Lifan!

Caixia　Hey, may I ask you a question on behalf of everyone? When can we have your wedding candies?

[Lanlan and Lifan look at each other, turning their heads shyly.

Zhang Qiye　Since they don't say anything, let's ask Director Xie. Director Xie, can you tell us the date? You are our Director and the Secretary of the Party Committee, you must tell us.

Director Xie　It's up to them when they have their baby. But the wedding day can be chosen on the day when the road of Jinfeng Tree Farm is completed. Then we can drive cars to send the couple into the bridal chamber! What do you think about it?

Everybody　Good!

Caixia　Shall I suggest the bridegroom-to-be and bride-to-be sing a piece of Huangmei Opera, Both Husband and Wife Return Home?

Everybody　OK!

Zhang Lanlan　(sing) The birds on the trees are in pairs,

Zhou Lifan　(sing) Mountains and water seem to smile.

Zhang Lanlan　(sing) I pick a flower near at hand,

Zhou Lifan　(sing) I wear it on my wife's hair.

章兰兰　(唱)从今金凤林场景色美,

周立凡　(唱)一路春风到家园。

章兰兰　(唱)千亩茶林枝叶飘香,

周立凡　(唱)十里花溪瓜果鲜。

章兰兰　(唱)你我好比春前草,

合　唱　(唱)播撒绿色满人间。

众　人　好!

[哑婶拿着一份报纸匆匆上,做动作示意是刚送来的,上边有植树造林的内容,兰兰接过报纸,眼前一亮。

章兰兰　(念)我们既要绿水青山,也要金山银山,而且绿水青山就是金山银山!

周立凡　(念)绿水青山就是金山银山!

众　人　(念)绿水青山就是金山银山!

合　唱　风雨过后见彩虹,

水更碧来山更青。

人人栽下一棵树,

神州处处有绿荫。

[光渐收。

——全剧终——

Zhang Lanlan (sing) From now on the tree farm's beautiful,

Zhou Lifan (sing) All the way home is springlike.

Zhang Lanlan (sing) The tea forest smells fragrantly,

Zhou Lifan (sing) The fruits are fresh over ten miles.

Zhang Lanlan (sing) You and me are like spring grass

(chorus) To spread green all over the world.

Everybody Good!

[Yashen hurries up with a newspaper, gesturing thatt his just delivered newspaperhas contents about afforestation on it. Lanlan takes the newspaper, her eyes becoming bright.

Zhang Lanlan (read) We want lucid waters and lush mountains as well as invaluable assets, and lucid waters and lush mountains are invaluable assets!

Zhou Lifan (read) Lucid waters and lush mountains are invaluable assets!

Everybody (read) Lucid waters and lush mountains are invaluable assets!

(Chorus) The rainbow comes after a storm,

With lucider water and lusher mountains.

If everyone can plant a tree,

Green shade is everywhere in China.

[Light fades away.

——The end——

注释 Notes

1.哭鼻子:A Chinese humorous expression with the meaning of crying.

2. 穆桂英: A fictional typical heroine in *The Generals of the Yangs*, a Chinese popular novel in the Ming Dynasty, who is often used as a proxy for a courageous and capable young woman in China.

3. 急着去砍头: A cursing expression in Anqing dialect to blame somebody who is in a great hurry to do something, which is considered by others as unnecessary. According to Buddhism, beheading was a Chinese death penalty in the past which should be imposed at the noon, otherwise, the soul of the criminal cannot be reborn after death.

4.唐伯虎点秋香:A famous comedy which is the 1993 Hong Kong Film Annual Box Office Champion, produced by Win's Movie Production Ltd. in Hongkong, directed by Zhou Xingchi and Li Lidao, starring Zhou Xingchi, Gong Li and Zheng Peipei. The film tells the story of Tang Bohu, one of the Four Gifted Scholars in the lower reaches of Changjiang River, who falls in love at first sight with Qiuxiang, the most beautiful maid of the rich and powerful Huas. With the help of the boatman, Tang Bohu uses a strategy to work as a servant for the Huas'. After some twists and turns, Tang Bohu succeedes in selecting Qiuxiang from 72 maids and finally marries her.

5. 三牲圆子——硬上: This is a Chinese two-part allegorical saying in the slang of Tongcheng in which 三牲圆子 is a kind of delicious pelleted food made from chopped fish, chicken, pork or beef, mutton, pork etc. In the area of Tongcheng city, which can satisfy guests' desire for good food so that it is hard for them to feel hungry. The saying means that a person tries every means to satisfy his or her desire regardless of others' feelings or emotions.

6.乌龟爬上秤——自称: This is a Chinese two-part allegorical saying which says that a turtle crawls on a steelyard to measure itself. The saying metaphorically means that one sings high praise for oneself.

7. 屙泡尿照照: A Chinese common saying to satirize somebody who has a high opinion of himself or herself.

8. 小妹:An appellation in Anqing dialect, referring to a young woman.

9. 挨熊: A Chinese expression with the meaning of being severely rebuked.

10. 打牙祭: A Chinese expression which, originally referring to eating a meal with meat dishes at the beginning and middle of a month, means eating a hearty meal occasionally.

11. 拉下水: A Chinese expression with the meaning of making an accomplice of somebody.

12. 吃盐长大的：A Chinese expression with the meaning of being experienced.

13. 过了这个村，就没有那个店：A Chinese proverb with the meaning that opportunities are rare and should not be missed.

14. 不做和尚头不冷：Buddhist monks should shave their heads, so their heads may feel cold. In Anqing dialect, the saying means that only those people know the difficulties in what they have experienced.

15. 打退堂鼓：This is a Chinese idiom. Originally it meant that drums played when feudal officials withdrew from their courts. Now it is a metaphor for backpedaling in the middle of something.

16. 兰桥会：The heterograph of 蓝桥会, the title of one of the 72 typical operettas of early Huangmei Opera, which tells a story about two young people falling in love at first sight at a bridge called Blue Bridge.

17. 诸葛草庐：The thatched cottage of the mastermind Zhu Geliang who later became the Prime Minister of the Shu State in the Three Kingdoms Period.

18. 货色：A derogatory expression to refer to a person, a thought, a work of literature, etc.

19. 水不惊，鱼不跳：A metaphorical saying with the meaning of "without any fuss".

20. 一团乱麻：A metaphor describing a lot of complex things.

21. 出气胎：A Tongcheng dialect similar to 出气筒, meaning "punching bag".

22. 横挑鼻子竖挑眼：A Chinese expression with the meaning of "being picky".

23. 惯子不孝,肥田出瘪稻：A Chinese common saying which means that Children who are too spoiled will be unfilial to their parents when they grow up, just like a field where too much fertilizer is put in will have shrivelled ears.

24. 旁观者清：A Chinese idiom which means that the onlooker see the game best.

25. 越俎代庖：A Chinese idiom which means that the officiant stepped over the altar to serve in the place of the cook. It is a metaphor for going beyond one's line of business to take care of someone else's business.

26. 人长树大：A metaphorical Chinese idiom which means that a child has grown up.

27. 重男轻女：A Chinese feudal thought that values men and despises women.

28. 含在嘴里怕化掉,不捧在手上不放心：An expression similar to 含在嘴里怕化掉,捧在手里怕摔了, in Chinese colloquialism, which means "to be fond of something and cherish it very much". It is usually used to describe the feelings of parents who love their children very much.

29. 手心手背都是肉：A Chinese common saying which literally means "both the palm and the back of the hand are made of flesh". Later it is used figuratively to mean that both are of equal importance.

30. 狐狸精：A Chinese expletive referring to a seductive woman.

31. 人肉搜索：Cyber Manhunt.

32. 贵姓：A Chinese term of respect to ask for a person's surname.

33. 免贵：A Chinese modest way to answer the polite question of asking for a person's surname.

34. 美人计：One of the thirty-six strategies, the trick of using beautiful women to lure people into traps.

35. 学雷锋：Lei Feng, a Chinese heroic soldier, was well-known for his helpfulness, devotion and selflessness. On August 15, 1962, he died on duty at the age of 22. In 1963, Chairman Mao Zedong called on Chinese people to learn from Lei Feng. Since then, Chinese people have taken part in the activities to learn from Lei Feng. In the minds of most Chinese people, learning from Lei Feng means helping others.

36. 婆媳守寡——没工夫：This is a Chinese two-part allegorical saying which says both a mother-in-law and a daughter-in-law are widowed, so there is no father-in-law（公公）and husband（丈夫）in the family. In the second part of the saying, 工 is homophonic for 公 and 夫 is homophonic for 丈夫. In Chinese language, 工夫 means free time, so this saying metaphorically means no free time.

37. 爆竹店失火——自己恭贺：This is a Chinese two-part allegorical saying which says that a firecracker shop catches fire,

which detonates the firecrackers, sounding like celebrating oneself. This saying makes fun of people boasting about themselves, or complimenting each other among family members.

38. 千千结: Originating from "The heart is like a double wire mesh, with thousands of knots in it" (心似双丝网,中有千千结) which is a line of the Ci poem "Thousands of Years · The Voices of Cuckoo" (《千秋岁 · 数声鶗鴂》) written by Zhang Xian, a poet of the Song Dynasty. Later it metaphorically means a lot of problems.

39. 天时人事日相催: A line in the poem "The Day Before the Winter Solstice" (《小至》) written by Du Fu, a poet in the Tang Dynasty. It means that time and affairs change quickly every day.

40. 同花: Several cards of the same suit in poker playing.

41. 顺子: Five consecutive cards of the same suit in poker playing.

42. 二百五: A Chinese colloquial expression, referring to people who are not only stupid and silly, but also stubborn and reckless.

43. 二: The abbreviated form of 二货, a Chinese colloquial expression with three meanings. The first refers to a stupid person, the second refers to someone who is not good at something, and the third refers to a silly but lovely person.

44. 卫生口罩——嘴上一套: This is a Chinese two-part allegorical saying which is used to satirize those people who are inconsistent in their words and deeds.